BALL AND POWDER

BALL AND POWDER

JOSHUA ROBERTSON

Echoic Mobile Press

Crimson Edge Press

Many thanks to Kildrak, Beans, Nickl, and the rest of the gang (including the most-patient gamemaster) who added to the story fodder that resulted in the creation of Ball and Powder. Ham certainly enjoyed every moment of our reckless and rowdy expeditions.

Not only do I hope for many more adventures to come in ridding fantastical worlds of the evil haunting them, but may each of you conquer the darkness in your own lives as well.

Contents

I

Rebirth

DAY 162, 4023 CE

Ham slanted his worn blunderbuss at the paltry human bastard and swelled his chest. Lifting the parcel of blood leaf in his free hand, he thundered, "You're two grams light! I swear if you snorted it yourself, I'll rattle your bone cage with lead."

He underscored his words with an agreeable, deep-throated *mm-hmm* as though the gods inscribed his testimony in one of those darned scripture books.

Blood leaf

The processed powder of a relatively common flower in grassland regions, usually bright red, leaving a stain around the mouth and nose of users. Powerful stimulant but incredibly addictive, usually highly illegal

---

+10 Speed, +2 Melee Damage, Duration 1 hour

Having no memory of how or when he entered the shop-keeper's home, Ham stifled a groan. A buzz, like suspended airships, reverberated in the back of his skull. He could not be certain if the sound came from the lack of drugs in his blood-stream or the fact that he had been reincarnated on Moravan moments ago. He did not remember how he died last, but the lingering memory of a flash of light and the smell of gunpow-der told him he likely met his end with a twin-barreled pis-tol pressed between his eyes. Little else could have taken him down.

The human clicked his tongue, standing up straight be-hind his counter. "You don't have enough *chips*, minotaur, and your horns are already spent. If you need work, I have a num-ber of jobs well suited for a champion of your stature."

Ham shoved his gun into its holster and eased his hand up to touch his hardened skull where his horns should have pro-truded from either side of his head. To his surprise, he rubbed flattened stumps—he must have had them hacked off during his last life.

Champion. The word rang between his wedge-shaped ears. Not all creatures on Moravan were created equal. Champions were adventurers with the ability to gain experience and skills, unlike this useless non-player character (NPC) stand-ing before him. Killing the bastard would only put a bounty on his head and alter his alignment. Any other day, he might splatter the human's brains with a swift headbutt, but this was the first day of his life. Again.

Shaking away the fuzz at the corners of his eyes, Ham twisted away from the NPC and manifested his stat sheet. His chest tightened, and the back of his head numbed as the glimmering yellow box emerged in the space in front of his eyes.

HAMROGENI "HAM" HERDSTOMPER			LEVEL 1	0/1000
MEDIUM	MINOTAUR	BARBARIAN	NEURTRAL GOOD	'150
POWER	16		HP	14/14
DEXERTITY	14		ARMOR	12
ENDURANCE	14			
INTELLIGENCE	6		SKILLS	SPELLS
AWARENESS	8		INTIMIDATE	IDENTIFY
CHARISMA	4		SURVIVAL	MARKSMAN
LUCK	2		SEAFARING	
DEFECT	BLOOD LEAF ADDICTION		CHIPS	5

He curled his lip in disappointment.

A handful of his ability scores were notable for a first-level champion, but the rest were laughable at best. He may not be the prettiest thing roaming the countryside nor the brightest flash of gunpowder, but you could throw him into any maze of tunnels blindfolded and he could navigate them. He silently took note of his hit points (HP), armor, skills, and spells, knowing they would be worthwhile once he went out to grind for experience.

His stat sheet listed his affinity for blood leaf as a defect. He hated that word: *defect*. Blood leaf was nothing less than red-powdered gold, boosting his power and endurance during a battle; so what if he liked the feeling of invulnerability? While some champions wanted greater influence or even fame, Ham lived to dungeon crawl, score chips, and snort blood leaf.

As Ham braced himself to engage with the shopkeeper

once more, the old wooden door of the place swung open. He lowered his eyes to a gnome lass with wide eyes and a nervous smile. Everything from her hair to her tiny boots was black as pitch, including the hilts of the daggers lining either side of her belt. He scoffed, suspecting she couldn't reach his waist even if she were given a stepstool, let alone cut his throat with those pigstickers.

Her eyes locked onto him as soon as she slipped through the crack.

"Hamrogeni, you're back!" she squealed in excitement, rushing forward to wrap her hands around his leg.

He jerked back in shock, hoping she might release her grip, but she clung tighter. Fighting the urge to shake her off and pull his gun, he asked, "I reckon I am s'posed to know you?"

She gave him a gentle pat behind his knee, then craned her neck to look up at him. "Still working your way through the character creation fog, huh? It will come back to you soon enough, along with our backstories." She grinned so wide, Ham thought her face could split in two. She finally stepped away, slapping her hands together. "Come on, Ham! I am Nickl of Clan Paddiwackle. You worked for my father. You keep me safe. Here, look!"

With a quick wave of her hand, she made her stat sheet visible to him.

NICKL NACKL			LEVEL 1	0/1000
SMALL	GNOME	ROGUE	CHAOTIC NEUTRAL	'75

POWER	6		HP	7/7
DEXERTITY	16		ARMOR	8
ENDURANCE	8			
INTELLIGENCE	12		SKILLS	SPELLS
AWARENESS	14		INVESTIGATE	-
CHARISMA	12		SNEAK	-
LUCK	4		EXPLOSIVES	

DEFECT	*EASILY FRIGHTENED*	CHIPS	40

His memories stitched themselves together almost as soon as Nickl flashed the yellow box into the space between them. Her late father, Penn Nackle, had owned one of the largest fleets of merchant ships in eastern Moravan at the southern tip of Squall's End, where they were now located. Ham had sailed and delivered goods for him for years as an NPC before Penn's demise slotted him and Nickl both into champion roles. Now they were fighting to earn their NPC status again.

"I reckon it's coming back to me, *mm-hmm*," Ham said. "We are going to do better this time."

"Did you purchase your powder yet?" Nickl asked, swiping her stat sheet away.

"Two doses," Ham sourly replied. "I got but half the chips you are holding."

"Mister Sammich," Nickl said, scooting past Ham toward the shopkeeper, "give me five more hits of blood leaf. He is going to need enough to carry him through the week."

"You don't have enough chips for five," Mister Sammich replied, "but I can give you four."

Nickl batted her eyes and interlaced her fingers before

placing her hands on the counter. "Oh no, Mister Sammich, you will give me five doses for the price of four."

The shopkeeper's eyebrows angled in surprise, and then he smiled. "Of course, Miss Nackle. Your father was a fine man. We all grieve his loss. Kirkwall is worse off without him. I would be happy to oblige, but," Mister Sammich leaned inward and whispered to Nickl, "if I may be so bold, I kindly suggest you find better company in which to travel. The wrong sort can smear your father's good name."

Ham could feel the heat rising from his neck to his ears at the clear insult. NPC or no, he might have to headbutt this man's brains down to his balls.

Nickl only laughed. "Oh, you mistake my father, Mister Sammich. He was a liar, a cheat, and an ass. His so-called fortune was seized by the bank to pay his debtors before he was buried. I am afraid I will have to make a new name for Nackle."

Mister Sammich dipped his cleft chin to his chest and nervously reached for the blood leaf packets under the counter. He lay them out as chips magically evaporated out of Nickl's coin purse. "All the same. Be careful of who you trust in Moravan. One man's friend is another man's enemy."

"What in tarnation does that mean?" Ham growled as Nickl retrieved the blood leaf and transferred it to Ham's inventory.

"Oh, nothing much," Mister Sammich said. "Just need to be aware that danger lurks where you least expect it."

"I always expect it," Ham retorted.

"He is postulating hollow warnings to keep us talking. He is just wasting our time to keep us from reaching our next level," Nickl said. "Stop talking to him or he will start repeating the same information."

"We haven't chosen any quests yet," Ham said.

"I picked up one while I was waiting for you to incarnate again. We are traveling south of Kirkwall to investigate a pestilence on a few farms," she said, her face diminishing in color. "I am hoping it isn't a death-dealer.

2

The Farm

DAY 162, 4023 CE

Ham hooted with bliss, rubbing the particles of red dust from his enlarged nostrils with a thick finger. The bright residue stained his grayish-brown fur, but he hardly noticed. The euphoric sensation that filled him nearly stole his breath, silencing the buzzing sound in his head. He was ready for a fight.

"There's the farm, Ham," Nickl said at his side, pointing her thin finger. "Do you see the black film covering the wheat? I can almost smell the death."

"*Mm-hmm.*" Ham rested his meaty hand on the blunderbuss hanging from the holster at his side and scanned the landscape. The crop was wilting and worthless, and the muck covering the yield gave off some sort of murky vapor. "Whatever it is, let's hope it's not catching. Who did you receive this quest from?"

"A stranger lurking outside Mister Sammich's shop," Nickl answered. "I did not catch his name, but he said we could see the magistrate for a reward after we completed clearing the pestilence."

"Sounds about right."

"You think it's a death-dealer?" Nickl asked.

Ham pulled his blunderbuss free and cocked the hammer. The blood leaf was coursing through his veins now. He was lighter on his feet, his muscles were swelling, and his skin was numb. "Only one way to find out."

He started down the hill toward the field, his hooves sinking into the softened earth with every heavy footfall. The northern wind whistled in his ears, carrying the stench of the rot with it.

The skeletal hand that tore through the ground twenty-five paces ahead hardly surprised him, nor did the half dozen that followed suit half a breath later. He expected something as frail as undead minions for low-level champions like themselves. Without so much as flinching, he lifted his arm and twisted his body to take aim, firing a slug at the ghastly extended appendage. And missed.

"Hellfire!" he boomed.

Nickl cried out after him, pulling the daggers from either side of her belt. "Someone fertilized this ground with the dead!"

The first skeleton lumbered forward and wildly swung at Ham, missing by almost an arm's length. A second one rushed Nickl, but she was ready. The lithe gnome-girl slashed the skeleton across the chest with her dagger. The undead creature exploded on impact, sending shards of bone in all directions.

Without warning, a bullet zipped by Ham and tore

through the skeleton's elongated skull with mastered precision. Skeleton parts sprayed in every direction, bouncing harmlessly off Ham's chest. He turned to identify the shooter and discovered a dwarf with a long rifle kneeling sixty paces to his rear.

A twinkle flashed in the long-bearded gent's blue eyes as he reloaded the weapon. He did not say a word, nodding to the undead stumbling over the withered grass.

Ham fired again and missed. "Horseshit!" He threw the weapon to the ground. Two rounds wasted with these industrially advanced boomsticks. He missed the days where cracking skulls involved the literal cracking of skulls.

The five remaining skeletons rushed him. Claws raked through the air. He twisted and turned, dodging the first four attacks with ease. The last skeleton, however, circled behind him and ripped through his shirt and flesh in one fluid blow. He howled in agony as 6 HP were shed from his maximum health.

"No!" Nickl screeched. She leaped forward to stand on the opposite side of the skeleton, gaining the upper hand with her attack. She separated the vertebrae between the shoulder blades of the undead monster, destroying it on impact.

The dwarf fired a second time from a distance and blew a skeleton to smithereens.

Ham roared, realizing only three skeletons remained, and he had done little more than scowl with his ugly mug. Eyeing the bony bastard directly in front of him, Ham stepped forward and cracked his head into the weaker enemy, caving in its skull from its nose to its eye sockets. The undead exploded.

Ham then rotated to the left and knocked the skeleton near Nickl back five feet.

The skeleton immediately advanced again, attacking and missing. Ham swatted away the other skeleton's attack too, hoping Nickl and the stranger could end this so he could see the damage done on his stat sheet.

"Let's get stabby!" Nickl did not miss a beat, gaining on the skeleton he had shoved a moment ago. Her daggers smashed through the back of the skeleton's skull, killing it instantly.

The dwarf, again, did not miss his mark with an impressive headshot to the last undead. He was already standing up and giving Ham a nonchalant thumbs up as the bullet soared mid-flight. The skeleton was lifted off its feet in slow motion, detonating into bone dust as Ham squinted at the cocky dwarf.

"What's your name, son?"

The dwarf loaded his rifle as he ambled down the hill. "Well...my friends call me Kildrak."

"What about non-friends?"

Kildrak scrunched his dark beard into his darker mustache. "I suppose they don't call me anything."

Ham squinted at the dwarf, wondering why he would have specified *friends* then.

"What about you?" he asked. "Do you two have names?"

"Of course we have names." Nickl laughed. "This is Hamrogeni Herdstomper but you can call him Ham, and I am Nickl Nackle of Clan Paddiwackle. Did the stranger outside Mister Sammich's send you to check out the farm too?" Nickl asked.

The dwarf waggled his head. "Nah, I haven't met a Mister Sammich. I was simply passing by and saw you and him gearing up for a wicked fight. I thought I'd lend a few bullets."

Ham glanced over his shoulder at the dispersed bones of the *dead* undead. Nickl mumbled her thanks and set off to dig through the hollowed graves and the remains for loot.

"I reckon it's best you stopped," Ham said. "Where are you heading now?"

"I have nowhere in mind. If it is all the same to you, I can tag along and get a few more chips. I am hoping to send some coin back home to my family," Kildrak said. "Besides, whatever you are tracking here looks like a core quest line. The experiences will be aplenty."

Ham crossed his arms. Adding members to the party meant he had to split winnings three ways, but they would certainly live longer with the dwarf among their number. Might even reach heroic status this time and then make their way back to being NPCs.

He missed the life of an NPC.

"Let me see your stat sheet," he said.

KILDRAK TORUNN			LEVEL 1	250/1000
MEDIUM	DWARF	MARKSMAN	CHAOTIC GOOD	'170
POWER	10		HP	10/10
DEXERTITY	10		ARMOR	10
ENDURANCE	16			
INTELLIGENCE	8		SKILLS	SPELLS
AWARENESS	12		PERCEPTION	-
CHARISMA	6		SHARPSHOOTER	-
LUCK	4		HISTORY	
DEFECT	FEMALE NPCS		CHIPS	125

Ham bristled at the dwarf's superior scores in endurance and awareness, then eyeballed the hefty number of chips in his purse. He had more than Ham and Nickl when they reincarnated.

Ham saw Nickl climbing out of one of the graves. "Did you find any chips?"

"I found 123 and already distributed them evenly between us. Check your sheet," Nickl said. She grinned at the dwarf. "I also went ahead and shared our quest with Kildrak. He is coming with us, right?"

"Yeah," Ham said brusquely, pulling up his updated stat sheet. He could not believe how little experience the skeletons had granted him. Kildrak had five times as much; the dwarf must have done some adventuring before running into them.

HAMROGENI "HAM" HERDSTOMPER			LEVEL 1	50/1000
MEDIUM	MINOTAUR	BARBARIAN	NEURTRAL GOOD	'150
POWER	16		HP	12/14
DEXERTITY	14		ARMOR	12
ENDURANCE	14			
INTELLIGENCE	6		SKILLS	SPELLS
AWARENESS	8		INTIMIDATE	IDENTIFY
CHARISMA	4		SURVIVAL	MARKSMAN
LUCK	2		SEAFARING	
DEFECT	BLOOD LEAF ADDICTION		CHIPS	46

Seeing his own hit points depleted, Ham remembered the gash across his back. While champions had the ability to quickly heal during a restful night, he did not want to go to sleep yet. Not only had the adventure scarcely begun, but his first dosage of blood leaf was still strong. Ham had the option of unearthing some liquid blue to drink down, finding a champion or NPC with skills in the magical arts, or pressing forward and bashing more skulls.

Liquid blue

A smooth blend of healing herbs typically found in open fields or mountainous regions.

+3d4 hit points when consumed

Kildrak stood behind Nickl silently as she rubbed her hands together. "What now, Ham? Are you okay to keep going?"

"*Mm-hmm*, I can shake it off," Ham replied, picking up his blunderbuss and reloading it. "We need to find the nearest farmhouse and gather some information."

"Well...the nearest homestead is back over the hill," Kildrak said. He adjusted his brown trench coat, showing multiple empty holsters on either side of his belt. "I did not stop on account of several undead bumbling around outside. I figure whoever lives there has joined the walking corpses, but you might find some clues to the cause of all this. A journal or dead body or something."

"That sounds like the beginnings of the breadcrumb trail we are looking for," Nickl said. "Should we check it out?"

"I cannot think of a better place to start." Ham grunted. "Let's hurry before these drugs run out."

He picked up his pace, climbing the hill from where Kildrak had come.

"Drugs?" Kildrak lifted his voice from the rear.

"Blood leaf," Nickl said. "It is Ham's elixir for life."

"Ah," Kildrak said.

Ham looked over his shoulder. "Do you have any on you?"

Kildrak shook his head. "I never touched the stuff but, uh, to each their own."

They raced over the hill and across a short sward to a two-story farmhouse sitting in front of another failing wheat field. The black muck weighed down the crops, putting out a putrid odor, but the state of the field was the least of Ham's concerns. A dozen and a half undead, a mixture of zombies and skeletons, roamed around the outskirts of the homestead. He could not imagine how many more might be tarrying inside.

Luckily, with a couple hundred feet separating them from the throng of ghouls, they had not been noticed yet.

"I reckon you didn't see anyone living among them during your first pass?" Ham asked.

"Not a soul. Like I said, I think whoever lived here is long gone. Might find him stumbling around in the mix," Kildrak answered, unstrapping his long rifle from his back.

"Y'all ready for a fight?" Ham swelled his chest.

"Not sure rampaging through is going to help us here, Ham," Nickl said. "A couple good hits will respawn us back to Mister Sammich with our stat sheets wiped."

"Don't you have a gunpowder bomb in that pouch of yours?" Ham asked, nodding at Nickl's satchel.

The gnome widened her eyes and cleared her throat before speaking in a high-pitched tone. "I have one. I couldn't afford enough materials to make more than that. I thought I would save it for a boss."

"We need the experience," Ham growled.

Kildrak lifted his eyebrow. "They are spread a bit thin to be using explosives."

Ham moved past Nickl and Kildrak, climbing the hill to get a better vantage point. He heard the whines and wails of the undead zigzagging around the farmstead below. Any fiends who might have taken notice of them lost interest and ventured in another direction.

"We need to search the farmhouse," Kildrak said, his heavy footsteps thudding behind Ham, "but nothing says we have to kill them all. Let's keep the bomb for a bigger fight."

Nickl whispered, her voice shaking, "I suppose I could sneak into the house."

"Let me draw them away first," Kildrak offered, lifting his gun a bit off his shoulder.

"Hold on, y'all. I am not letting Nickl go into that house alone," Ham snorted. "Who knows how many undead are roaming inside?"

"If you are down there stomping around inside the house, even my shooting will not distract them. Nickl can get in and out without making much more than a peep," Kildrak argued.

Ham rubbed his nose, eyeing Kildrak with disdain. The dwarf may be right, but he would rather they all be incarnated again than have Nickl restart at Mister Sammich's inn without him. He was not about to let her get cornered.

"If you think I am just going to sit up here while she is tiptoeing through the house and you are blasting bastards," Ham growled, "you're crazier than a run-over coon. My place is at her side."

Kildrak scrunched his face and finally relented. "Alright.

But let them come away from the house before you head down."

"*Mm-hmm*. Get on, then," Ham said.

Kildrak tugged on his dark beard before heading back the way they had come, circling around the outskirts of the farmhouse. At the same time, Ham and Nickl trekked in the opposite direction to put some distance between them. In short time, Kildrak's gunshots were echoing across the decaying fields.

The undead started ambling toward the dwarf on the other side of the field. Ham took a moment to find Kildrak kneeling in the mud. He fired his gun, retreated backwards several feet, and repeated the pattern.

Once the lumbering corpses were a couple hundred feet beyond the farmhouse, Nickl whispered, "Let's go."

Ham was naturally faster than the gnome and even swifter with the blood leaf pumping in his veins, but he still stayed behind Nickl until they were at the rear door of the house.

Nickl paused on the doorstep, her wide eyes looking up at him. "I hear movement inside. You better go first. No guns."

"*Mm-hmm*," Ham rumbled, wrapping his meaty hand around the knob and swinging the door open. A zombie stood immediately on the opposite side of the door. No sooner did it whip around than Ham split its head open with his own skull. The monster thudded to the ground.

Banging resounded upstairs followed by another gunshot outside.

"I reckon you better find whatever we are looking for," Ham said, scanning the standard kitchen decorated with pictures and dishtowels portraying a variety of domesticated cattle. He frowned. "Tarnation. This farmer sure as hell got what was comin' to him."

Nickl scooted around him to an entryway leading to a sitting room of sorts. "Ham, now is not the time to talk about your lesser evolved cousins."

"*Mm-hmm.*" He stayed behind her. The larger room looked to be ransacked with tipped over end tables, a mud-stained rug, and scattered papers and books strewn over a corner desk. A faded staircase to Ham's left trailed upstairs. Near the base, another door against the far wall led back outside. Ham kicked a lamp to the side and watched Nickl move toward the desk.

"I bet I can find something in all these papers and books," she said.

Uneven footsteps pounding down the stairs caught Ham's attention. A thick zombie wearing a cowboy hat, skin hanging from its grisly bones, clambered down the steps in cowboy boots.

Ham cracked his knuckles. "You keep looking. I am going to give this farmer a whaling that will haunt him into his next life."

He met the farmer at the base of the stairs when the farmer flipped up a six-gun and fired. Lead tore through Ham, burning like hellfire.

Fighting the impulse to look at his stat sheet and check the full damage, he took solace in knowing he was still standing. Gritting his teeth like he could bite the sites off the farmer's gun, he headbutted the undead cow handler. He heard the skull crack, but the farmer maintained his ground, so Ham shoved him back up the stairs for good measure.

The cowboy fired again. The bullet whizzed by Ham's ear and tore into the plaster behind him.

Gunshots fired frantically outside the house.

Nickl shouted, "All the gunfire is bringing the undead back this way, Ham!"

"Find our clue!" Ham growled, stepping up two stairs and crashing his skull forward again, cracking the farmer's face in two and knocking off his wide-brimmed hat. Still, the lanky bastard stood in those cotton-picking boots.

Another shot from the six-shooter barreled by Ham, missing by a hair. His luck was not going to hold out.

"I found it! I found a map, Ham!" Nickl cried. "And a liquid blue."

"Good." Ham flipped up his blunderbuss from his belt and pressed it to the farmer's chest. The slug burst through the body, dropping the undead bastard. Ham picked up the farmer's gun with a snort. "We best skedaddle. *Mm-hmm.*"

3

Burning Daylight

DAY 164, 4023 CE

Another day. Another city. The same NPC.

Ham was not surprised to find that Mister Sammich had spawned from Kirkwell to Clery to peddle his wares. He expected the shopkeeper to continue popping up at every trading post from here on out, until Ham was slain and respawned or he reached a high enough level to become an NPC again. He wished champions could fast travel across the map like NPCs. The ability to adventure faster meant they would gain experience quicker which, subsequently, might allow Nickl and him to quit their recurring lives as champions and regain NPC status.

HAMROGENI "HAM" HERDSTOMPER			LEVEL 1	950/1000
MEDIUM	MINOTAUR	BARBARIAN	NEURTRAL GOOD	'150
POWER	16		HP	14/14
DEXERTITY	14		ARMOR	12
ENDURANCE	14			
INTELLIGENCE	6		SKILLS	SPELLS
AWARENESS	8		INTIMIDATE	IDENTIFY
CHARISMA	4		SURVIVAL	MARKSMAN
LUCK	2		SEAFARING	
DEFECT	BLOOD LEAF ADDICTION		CHIPS	142

He knew the wish was impossible. Ham simply longed for the trouble-free life of a non-adventurer.

The shopkeeper offered a blank look as he exchanged blood leaf for the chips that Ham acquired over the past couple of days. While Ham examined his stat sheet, Nickl checked her inventory, acquiring a few more vials of liquid blue for the road ahead. Ham saw the rolled-up map they collected at the farm sticking out of her belt as she leaned in close to Mister Sammich to finish her purchase. Ham had not bothered to read the scratching on the parchment, trusting Nickl to get them where they needed to go.

"We are about finished up here. Where will we be heading off to now?" Ham asked her, stuffing his drugs into his pocket. They had walked nearly two days to reach Clery, surviving the usual random encounters, including wild animals, road bandits, and the occasional roaming monster. None were worth mentioning, but they provided enough experience and chips for Ham to stock up for the real fight.

"Next stop is Braewood Keep," Nickl said softly, rubbing

her small hands together. "We will collect Kildrak from the tavern and head northeast."

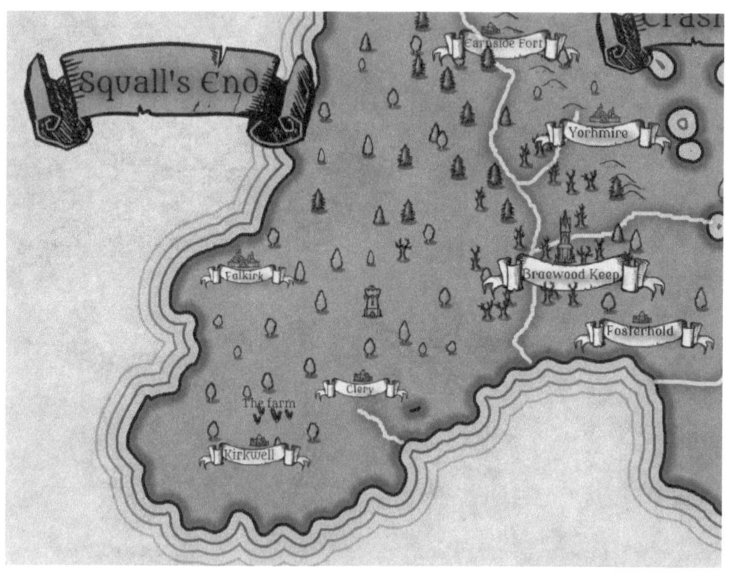

"Can't say I've ever seen a dwarf so quick to be paintin' his tongue with tarantula juice." Ham snorted air out of his large nostrils. "I'll admit he can shoot better than any chap I've seen, but he was askin' for the ol' lush-crib before we even reached the gates. I hope he is not a mop."

"I do not think he is a habitual drunk," Nickl said, catching his meaning. "If so, he would be sipping from a flask, wouldn't he?"

"*Mm-hmm.* I reckon."

"Braewood Keep, you say?" Mister Sammich hummed, not bothering to acknowledge anything they said of Kildrak. The shopkeeper scarcely looked at Ham since they approached, likely regretting what terrible things he said about Ham the last time they crossed. Instead, he kept a keen eye on Nickl. "If you want to go there, you will need a key to the front gates."

Ham stomped his foot. "Tarnation! I am guessing you don't have those lying around in your stock, *mm-hmm*? That's alright, Nickl. We can bust through the door." Ham flexed his arm, looking down on Mister Sammich. "Heck, I reckon this is the part where you send us wandering off on a side quest, *mm-hmm*? Alright, alright, I'll play your game."

"Let him talk, Ham." Nickl laughed. "Where do we get a key?"

Mister Sammich went on as though Ham had not said a word, speaking as though he were reading from a script. "Rumor has it that the keep has been abandoned for years, but the guard at Toonok Tower gives champions the means to test their might."

"The guard has the key? Where is Toonok Tower?" Ham asked.

"North," Mister Sammich said. "I will update your map."

Ham crossed his arms, feeling the weight of his blunderbuss hanging at his side. "We are going to travel across the whole of Squall's End before we see this death-dealer bite the ground. Best be avoiding NPCs on the road, or we are going to have more side quests than we have fingers and toes."

"Do not say *death-dealer*." Nickl shivered. "We do not know whether it is or not."

"*Mm-hmm*," Ham grumbled. "We had zombies and skeletons and an undead sodbuster bumbling about. What else could cause that except a death-dealer?"

Nickl gulped. "Let's go get Kildrak."

Leading the way through the streets, Nickl skipped alongside Ham until they reached the tavern at the edge of town where the dwarf was known to have gone. As they approached the steps leading to the double doors, Ham could hear the din of drunks hollering, glass shattering, and wood splintering. To him, it sounded like a fight was brewing inside. He reached out to stop Nickl from going through the swinging doors as a small gnome woman came rolling out head over heels.

Ham instinctively reached for his blunderbuss, seeing the number of guns the gnome was carrying on her. Standing at her back, he could see a twin-barreled shotgun hanging over either shoulder with a pepperbox rifle sticking out, angled between them in another holster. She also had a pair of crossed flintlock pistols in additional holsters at the small of her back. But the pair of black-eyed Susans dipped on either side of her belt were the immediate danger as she scrambled to her feet and pulled them free.

She pushed her golden hair from her eyes while grasping a six-shooter in her hand and then spit at the dirt. "You want to play rough? I'll shoots every last one of you!" She suddenly turned her head to see Nickl and Ham. Tilting her chin, she said, "You going to back me up in here or am I going to have to color the walls red on my own?"

"What?" Nickl asked, slack-jawed.

"Sure as a gun, this is the tavern brawl portion of the adventure." Ham shook his head and snorted. "Why can we never make it through the low levels without making a fuss at some random-ass rum-hole? I reckon that means you will be joining us after we knock some heads together."

"Will there be bad guys to shoots?" The gnome squinted at

him. "As long as I am shooting something, I will go wherever you go, muley."

Ham took a step back at the insult and corrected her. "My name is Hamrogeni Herdstomper, but you can call me Ham."

Nickl piped up beside him, brushing his hand off his blunderbuss. "And I am Nickl!"

The gnome spun the guns in either hand and then brought them to a swift halt with her fingers on the triggers. "Nickl and Ham, eh? Well, you can call me Beans."

BEANS			LEVEL 1	1250/1000
MEDIUM	GNOME	GUN ENTHUSIAST	CHAOTIC EVIL	'170
POWER	6		HP	14/18
DEXERTITY	14		ARMOR	10
ENDURANCE	8			
INTELLIGENCE	16		SKILLS	SPELLS
AWARENESS	10		PERCEPTION	-
CHARISMA	12		SHARPSHOOTER	-
LUCK	6		HISTORY	
DEFECT	*STEALING*		CHIPS	420

"Did you see a dwarf in there?" Nickl asked.

"Plenty," Beans said. The roar of the ruckus increasing inside resounded into the street. Several shots suddenly fired, a couple bullets raining through the windows. "A certain dwarf with a long rifle started this mess by teasing a servant girl who belonged to another man. After a few words, fists started flying."

Ham turned to Nickl with a sour look. "That'd be Kildrak. I thought he was off getting tangle-footed, not trying to be pirooting with a painted cat, *mm-hmm?*"

"Oh, you know him? He has not had a lick of whiskey," Beans said. "He is fully sober."

Ham grunted. More glass shattered inside as though someone were throwing bottles. "That really tans my hide. Guess we better save his bacon."

"I should not shoots him, then?" Beans asked.

Ham eyed Beans with concern, considering the gnome's strength, while Nickl briskly shook her head.

Reaching into his pocket, Ham took a sniff of his newly acquired blood leaf and rolled his shoulders back. The powder burned his nostrils, sending his heart into a frenzy. Without a word, he stamped his hooves up the wooden stairs and pushed open the doors with a gnome girl on either side of him.

The musky smell of gunpowder and whiskey filled Ham's nostrils as he scanned the wrecked room of the tavern. Tables were flipped. Bottles were broken. Bullet holes decorated the ceiling and walls. In one corner, he saw a group of patrons huddled away from the fighters, gulping on their drinks as though the liquid were evaporating from the glasses. Against the back wall, he found Kildrak held firmly by several humans. His face was bloody, his beard stained crimson. One of the ruffians shook his fist as though he had just finished clocking the dwarf across the jaw.

"Y'all picked the wrong place to get corned," Ham said, curling his hands into fists.

Beans did not wait for him to finish his threat, lifting both guns and shooting iron. Each bullet zipped by the crowd of men, tearing through the wall on the opposite end, one of which nearly hit Kildrak.

KILDRAK TORUNN			LEVEL 1	1250/1000
MEDIUM	DWARF	MARKSMAN	CHAOTIC GOOD	'170

POWER	10		HP	14/18
DEXERTITY	10		ARMOR	10
ENDURANCE	16			
INTELLIGENCE	8		SKILLS	SPELLS
AWARENESS	12		PERCEPTION	-
CHARISMA	6		SHARPSHOOTER	-
LUCK	4		HISTORY	
DEFECT	FEMALE NPCS		CHIPS	260

The dwarf's beady eyes widened in fear.

"We said don't shoot him!" Nickl shouted.

"I do not want any trouble! You all take your friend and get out of—" the bartender started shouting from behind the counter. Ham did not take the time to entertain the chump; he let the men beat up Kildrak but complained when they came to rescue him. He knew a good brawl when he saw one.

Ham charged forward at the first drunk, headbutting him in the face. The mop surprisingly kept his feet, even though the skin split over his left eye and blood immediately started gushing down his face.

"Kill 'em!" one of the men shouted, lifting his weapon to fire.

"Stop!" the bartender shouted again.

The gun tilted in Ham's direction, then dropped as Nickl scurried across the floor and planted her daggers in the man's gut. The deadly strike dropped him to the ground, where he would finish bleeding out.

Four shots echoed around Ham, each surprisingly missing him at short range, bespeaking the men's intoxication. Another round of bullets fired from Beans's guns, these two breaking up the floorboards by Ham's hooves.

"What in tarnation are you shooting at?" Ham twisted his neck at the gnome girl, who stumbled a bit. He had not noticed before, but she was as sozzled as the men they were fighting. "You are smashed! I have a mind to give you a licking too if you raise that iron again and shoot me, *mm-hmm*?"

"Calm down, muley," Beans said. "I promise I won't shoots you."

With a growl, Ham turned around and reached for the guy holding Kildrak. With little effort, he pulled him off and tossed him across the room. The guy he had headbutted a moment before weakly slugged him in the gut as Ham reached around him. With a grunt, he pulled up his stat sheet to see a life shredded off his hit points.

"You've got to be kidding me," he muttered, headbutting the guy a second time and dropping him like a sack of flour.

Nickl somersaulted to another drunk and cut him at the knees, while the men fired another round of their guns at them. Ham grunted as two bullets tore into him, hearing Beans squeal behind him as she was struck by lead too.

Ham could hear the bartender pleading from behind the bar. "Please—"

Pushing off the wall, Kildrak nodded his thanks to Ham and stomped down on his long rifle at his feet. The weapon flipped up into his arms and he fired at the back of the nearest man. The bullet blasted between the man's flailing arm and flannel shirt, nearly striking Ham.

Ham opened his mouth to protest Kildrak's terrible aim when Beans missed another shot, slinging a lead plumb between his legs. The second shot popped the guy Kildrak missed in the shoulder.

"If y'all cannot shoot, then put your guns away. Tarnation!" Ham screamed, jerking his blunderbuss out. Someone tugged at his arm—attempting to grapple him, no doubt. He twisted his gun at the fat human and pulled the trigger. The array of bullets hit true, blowing half the face off the poor bastard.

The fight stopped dead as the body toppled over and smashed to the floor.

"Ham," Nickl cleared her throat, "that was the bartender."

"Heck." Ham gritted his teeth and tensed his shoulders. Those who remained in the tavern stampeded past him and out the double doors into the road, shouting for the guard. Nickl, Beans, and Kildrak slogged to his side, staring at the twitching corpse at their feet.

"Well," Kildrak said, "this is not going to be good."

Ham turned on the dwarf. "What were you doing raisin' sand in here anyway? I thought you were getting a drink!"

"No. I would never drink," Kildrak said, his beard waggling as he talked. "I was buying some pretty ladies drinks."

"We are never supposed to kill the bartender, Ham," Nickl grimaced, jabbing her daggers back into the scabbards at her belt. "I think I leveled up."

NICKL NACKL			LEVEL 2	1100/3000
SMALL	GNOME	ROGUE	CHAOTIC NEUTRAL	'75

POWER	6		HP	13/13
DEXERTITY	16		ARMOR	8
ENDURANCE	8			
INTELLIGENCE	12		SKILLS	SPELLS
AWARENESS	14		INVESTIGATE	-
CHARISMA	12		SNEAK	-
LUCK	4		EXPLOSIVES	
DEFECT	*EASILY FRIGHTENED*		CHIPS	40

"I know." Ham slung his blunderbuss downward. Killing the bartender was going to negatively swing his alignment. He did not even want to look at his character sheet.

Beans laughed. "That was great. Are we going to shoots the guard now, muley?"

"I told you the name is Hamrogeni Herdstomper. You can call me Ham. And no, we are not killing the guard." Ham rubbed the dull edge of his cut-off horns. "I reckon we better get on out of town, *mm-hmm*. We are burning daylight anyhow."

4

Gone Sour

Tramping up the winding path to the Toonok Tower, Ham found the willpower to look at his stat sheet once more. Shaking his head, his eyes hovered over the new measure of his alignment after killing the bartender. The compass of his morality had shifted nearly fifty points, drifting him closer to an evil alignment. He could already feel his mind becoming more feral and chaotic.

HAMROGENI "HAM" HERDSTOMPER			LEVEL 2	1245/3000
MEDIUM	MINOTAUR	BARBARIAN	NEURTRAL GOOD	'105
POWER	16		HP	24/24
DEXERTITY	14		ARMOR	12
ENDURANCE	14			
INTELLIGENCE	6		SKILLS	SPELLS
AWARENESS	8		INTIMIDATE	IDENTIFY
CHARISMA	4		SURVIVAL	MARKSMAN
LUCK	2		SEAFARING	
			INTERCEPT	
DEFECT	BLOOD LEAF ADDICTION		CHIPS	182

"What did you say your name was again, muley?" Beans asked, looking over her shoulder at Ham. The golden-haired gnome smiled from ear to ear.

"My name is Hamrogeni Herdstomper, but you can call me Ham," he answered.

Kildrak sighed heavily at the rear. "She is teasing you, Ham. She has asked you the same question for three days."

"All the same," Ham's voice trailed off, swiping away his stat sheet and peering up at the sun hovering in the sky. Like Nickl, he had leveled up, gaining almost double the hit points. He also gained a new ability called Intercept, where he could interrupt an attack as an extra action if his adjacent ally was being shown aggression. He could not be excited, though, knowing his alignment was dipping downward. He wanted to regain his NPC status, but he could not be stuck as an evil NPC. Luckily, his level was low enough that it allowed him plenty of time to turn things around; he needed to do more good deeds!

Nickl fastened a bomb to her belt and then pointed to the tower at the top of the rise. Ham noticed she had crafted several more of her explosive devices while they marched along the road, making quite the display around her waist. "We are almost there. Let's make this quick so we can be on our way to Braewood Keep."

"I am praying we ain't barkin' at a knot," Ham said, twisting his neck to stare at the rocky ravines on either side of the path. If any of them stepped wrong, they would likely fall to their deaths. "I am not sure I trust Mister Sammich."

"I do not think we have anything to fear from him. He

is the quest-giver, Ham." Nickl covered her mouth to stifle a laugh.

Ham nodded. "Dang, I know that, but if you think about it, no champion would ever be in danger if it weren't for Mister Sammich sending them off on adventures."

"He has a point," Beans said.

"We would never gain experience or chips without him either," she countered.

"Also true," Beans replied.

"Well, Mister Sammich is the last thing we need to be worried over." Kildrak adjusted the long rifle over his shoulder. "We caused quite the disturbance back there, and not one guardsman has come after us. I expected a posse to come riding us down. No way we are going to get far without the bartender's death coming back to nip us in the rear."

The sudden sound of airships humming arose from the canyon behind the tower. Two large hunks of metal, shaped like sailing ships meant for the sea, rose with three whirring horizontal propellers extending at different lengths where sails should have been erected. A fourth push-propeller extended from the back of the airship to give it greater thrust.

"What in tarnation!" Ham glowered at Kildrak, who had seemingly willed the airships into existence. "Why did you have to say something? You never remind the *gods* of ill will due to us unless you want to bring on ruckus. Next time, keep your trap shut, *mmhmm*."

Kildrak frowned.

"Calm down, muley," Beans said. "We can handle them."

"Looks like the governor at Clery sent half their guard after us," Nickl said, pulling the bomb off her belt as quick as she had attached it.

Kildrak rocked his head from shoulder to shoulder, gaping in disbelief at the two gnomes. "We cannot fight airships. We are not high enough levels."

Several armored guards moved along the railing, adjusting their iron cannons and rifles. A captain could barely be seen standing farther back on the decks of the left-handed ship. His arms waved as he gave orders, shouting to the other ship in a somewhat frantic fashion.

Beans laughed at Kildrak's expression. "I'll shoots every one of them if it means I can get one of those cannons. You think you can carry it, muley?"

"We need the key inside that tower to finish our quest," Nickl said, trying to keep the group on track.

Ham ignored Beans, hovering his hand over his blunder-buss. "We are going to get in there, grab the key, and then skedaddle, *mmhmm.*"

Kildrak scoffed. "That easy, huh?"

"Like lickin' butter off a knife," Ham replied.

The boom of one of the cannons resounded as an iron ball flew over their heads and exploded against the path behind them.

"Move!" Ham ordered.

The four of them pushed up the path toward the entryway of the tower, where two guards were waiting with their guns drawn. Each fired, the bullets whizzing overhead. Kildrak stopped in his tracks and returned fire. His bullet ricocheted off the stone wall behind them.

"I'll shoots 'em!" Beans shouted, firing one of her black-eyed Susans. The shot was too high.

"We don't want to be killing any more guards," Ham shouted.

Another cannon fired.

"I got it," Nickl cried, chucking one of her bombs to intercept the hunk of iron. Hitting her mark, the cannonball struck the bomb and exploded in the air near the center of the tower. The explosion of gunpowder and shrapnel rocked the edifice, threatening to knock it over.

"Hellfire!" Ham yelled, lifting his arm protectively over his head.

"That was awesome!" Beans squealed.

Two more shots sounded from the guards. One of the bullets tore through Ham's arm; the other flew by, close to hitting the same mark. He felt his newly acquired hit points drain from his overall life.

He gritted his teeth, blood boiling. Stomping his hooves until he reached the nearest guard, he said, "We ain't looking for a fight. Give us the key to Braewood Keep and we will be on our way."

"We aren't giving you anything," the guard sneered, "save a stone bed behind bars."

Kildrak fired at the airship again. The bullet zipped well above the propellers as though he were giving a warning shot and not trying to hit anything. Beans, on the other hand, fired twice at the ship, striking a guard on either side of one of the cannons. Shouts echoed as Nickl reached Ham's side.

"Come on," she said to the guards sweetly, batting her eyelashes, "where is the key?"

The guard answered by lifting his gun to her face and firing. The bullet tore through her, blood spraying. Ham's heart stopped as Nickl stumbled, miraculously staying on her feet. If she had not reached a new level, she would have been six feet under. Even now, she looked to be hanging on by a thread.

The second guard lifted his gun too, but Ham used Intercept to swat the weapon to the side as he fired. With a snarl, Ham headbutted the first guard for maximum damage, denting his helmet into the frontal lobe of the bastard. Unlike Nickl, the guard's eyes bulged fully, and he fell to the dirt in a heap.

After saying they wouldn't kill guards, he robbed this one of his evening supper and every supper thereafter.

Served him right after shooting Nickl. He was better off as a compost pile.

Ham huffed to the second guard. "You're buzzard food."

Shots fired behind Ham between the airships and his other two companions, but Ham did not bother looking to see where the bullets fell. His vision was bleeding red.

Nickl retreated and downed a liquid blue from her inventory as the remaining guard lifted his weapon at Ham. Bracing himself, a lead bullet exploded through his gut, draining his life another handful of points.

"They are coming down from the airships!" Kildrak cried as several long ropes fell over the railings to the ground. Armored guards already started sliding down to intercept them.

"Hold them back." Ham clutched the guard in his meaty arms and started dragging him into the tower. The man's gun fell from his hands while attempting to fight against Ham's grip.

Nickl shouted at him as he stepped inside the hollowed pile of stones. "What are you going to do?"

"Just have a little chat!" Ham yelled back.

Gunfire boomed outside as the guards exchanged more gunfire with Beans and Kildrak. Ham heard Beans's victorious shout as she likely dropped one of the sentries.

His wounds burned painfully and his mind reeled with hateful thoughts as he tossed the guard into a table against the far wall. Slinging out his blunderbuss, he pointed the barrel at the unarmed guard's knees.

"I reckon I already asked you nicely to give me the key to Braewood Keep, *mmhmm*?" Ham curled his lip, intimidating the guard.

The man visibly shook in his boots, his blue eyes pinpointed on the deadly iron in Ham's hands. "I'll tell you anythi—"

Ham fired, the slug ripping through the man's left kneecap. His high-pitched scream echoed off the walls as he crumpled to the floor.

Ham reloaded. "Best say something smart before my turn comes 'round again or I will blast off your yam bag, *mmhmm*."

The tower suddenly rocked again as several cannonballs smashed through the walls, raining rocks in all directions. Ham lifted his eyes to see the inner walls swaying. The tower could very well cave in on him at any moment. More gunfire resounded beyond the entryway as his party gave him a few more seconds.

The guard spewed information, his hand sliding from his

knee to cover his crotch. "We do not have the key to Brae-wood Keep. It was stolen weeks ago by monsters led by a man smelling of death."

Ham held his action, squinting at the man squirming on the ground, wondering if he was lying to him. "You stretchin' the blanket?"

"What? No! I would never..." The guard fumbled, his eyebrows knitting together. "He wore all black, and his face was hidden in the shadows of his hood. He killed four men before snagging the key and heading east."

"What kind of monsters?" Ham asked.

"Undead. Half-rotting corpses that looked to have been hauled straight up from beneath their gravestones." The guard gulped. "And that is the straight truth. I swear it."

The death-dealer!

Nickl's scream distracted Ham—had she been seriously wounded? The sounds of gunfire intensified with more cannons exploding around the tower. The din was so deafening that Ham barely heard the guard's next words.

"That is all I know," he said. "Please let me live."

"I would like to," Ham snorted, feeling the itch of his altered alignment buzz in his head, urging him to pull the trigger, "but you shot me and my friends out there. So, like I said, you're buzzard food."

"No!" the guard roared, grasping at the air as though a weapon might magically appear.

Ham unloaded his blunderbuss again, splattering the guard's insides across the back wall. That was one less enemy he would have to worry about trailing behind them. He holstered his weapon and snorted.

Rushing out of the tower doorway, he searched for Nickl. He would do whatever he could to keep her from being reincarnated again.

Kildrak was the closest to him, bleeding from the shoulder, and Beans was right behind him, stumbling back with multiple injuries to boot. He heard a half dozen or more guards marching up from the rear. Ham scowled as bullets flew on either side of his horns, and he finally caught sight of Nickl hiding farther down the path from which they had come.

"What happened?" Nickl cried out to him, holding her bleeding face.

"The key was taken by the death-dealer," Ham answered, pulling at Kildrak and Beans as he passed. "Forget these bastards. We need to go east."

"If I am not getting a cannon, I am at least taking another rifle!" Beans shouted, scrambling by Ham to grab the weapon off the dead guard.

"What did you do to the other sentry?" Kildrak asked.

"Beefed him," Ham said. "I reckon he deserved a lot worse."

Kildrak frowned as Beans made her way back. "You are really muddying up the waters. Let's go."

5

The Eastern Road

DAY 169, 4023 CE

Ham narrowed his eyes to see through the puff of smoke emanating from the end of his blunderbuss and then strode forward to kick the carcass of the wolf with his hoof. The beast did not so much as whimper, the crimson color of its insides already soaking into its gray fur.

Beans slung the newly acquired rifle she stole from the dead guard at the tower over her shoulder. "Nice shooting, muley. I think it's the last of the howlers." She twisted around, pursing her lips at the handful of scattered wolves spread over the weaving dirt path leading through the grasslands.

"Yeah. Until another pack comes over one of these hills," Kildrak said. He crossed his thick arms over his chest and turned from the party. "How many wolves have we put down over the last couple of days? A dozen?"

"At least," Nickl replied, swiping her character sheet long enough to scrunch her face into a pout. Kildrak wandered up the path with a snort and shake of his head. Nickl sighed as he ambled off. "We have not been rewarded much for killing them either."

NICKL NACKLE			LEVEL 2	2150/3000
SMALL	GNOME	ROUGE	CHAOTIC GOOD	'75
POWER	6		HP	12/13
DEXERTITY	16		ARMOR	8
ENDURANCE	8			
INTELLIGENCE	12		SKILLS	SPELLS
AWARENESS	14		INVESTIGATE	-
CHARISMA	12		SNEAK	-
LUCK	4		EXPLOSIVES	
DEFECT	EASILY FRIGHTENED		CHIPS	220

"Of course we haven't," Ham said, turning his eyes from the dwarf. "They are not part of the main quest line. Besides, they are too low level to be much of a threat to us. We could nearly defeat the darn beasts with a sour look."

Beans hummed in her throat, reloading her gun. "I wish it were that easy. Unless we start skinning them and selling the pelts, they are not worth the cost to shoots them."

Ham reached for the pouch on his belt that held the slugs for his blunderbuss. He would run out of lead plumbs if he continued firing at this rate.

Nickl kicked at the dirt, complaining, "I am ready to be an NPC again. I feel like we have a long way until we can reclaim our non-champion status. Remember what it was like, Ham?" Nickl sighed, shoving her hands in her pockets. "Lounging around the estate, not thinking or saying much except whatever broken script was written on the tips of our tongues."

"*Mmhmm.*" He placed his large hand on her little shoulder.

"Tickles the back of my hide thinking about it. I reckon we will get back there someday, but first, we need to find this key to Braewood Keep."

A gunshot cracked from over the hill.

"Kildrak!" Nickl shouted, trying to rush forward, only to find her feet planted in place.

Ham snapped his attention to the sound, seeing that the dwarf had disappeared down the path. He was a good hundred paces beyond reach. Ham rumbled in his throat. "He has initiated combat. We are moving in rounds."

"He could be dead before we can reach him," Beans said. Then with a forced sniff, she reached for her six-shooters. "I will avenge him."

"He is not dead yet," Ham said. "Hang on."

Reaching for a bit of blood leaf, Ham inhaled the red powder in a mighty snort and then picked up the two gnomes in front of him. Nickl squealed and Beans wriggled as he scarpered to the top of the hill. With the drug surging through his bloodstream, his legs pumped like pistons, reaching the top of the hill before his round had come to an end. His chest burned from the strain of climbing the hill while carrying his companions. Nevertheless, he found the strength to position himself in preparation for a barrage of bullets and raked his eyes over the terrain.

No bullets came.

At the bottom of the hill, a frothing river roared by, splitting the land in twain, undoubtedly spilling into the sea a couple leagues southward. A few half-dead trees decorated the landscape, but they were not a quarter as ugly as the lumbering undead faltering along the bank. Skeletons and zombies alike staggered to and fro, most already meandering their way to Kildrak, who stood twenty paces ahead of Ham. One of the fiends stepped within striking range of the dwarf but did not have the momentum to make an attack.

"Put me down, muley," Beans demanded, trying to straighten her gun. "It is my shot."

Ham released her and Nickl in a flash, knowing he would not be able to smash anything for a bit. Beans fired almost as soon as her feet hit the ground, shooting the zombie in front of Kildrak. The hot iron ripped through the undead's chest. Nickl was next, rushing forward—skirting by the dwarf—and stabbing her dagger into the zombie's skull to finish it.

"Thanks," Kildrak huffed, turning to the mob coming at them. He fired his pepperbox rifle and hit another. "I do not know where they came from. The area was clear one moment and full of undead the next, almost like they *poofed* into existence."

Ham warily glanced at the monsters advancing on their position, fearful of asking the dwarf's meaning. Creatures could not emerge from nothing unless magic was afoot.

The ground shuddered under their feet, a putrid smell touching the edge of Ham's enlarged nostrils.

"Sweet mustard! What is that?" Beans asked, pointing across the river.

"Death-dealer," Nickl said frightfully under her breath, eyes widening. "*Ooo*, Ham, it *is* a death-dealer."

Ham gripped the handle of his blunderbuss and snapped his attention to a ghostly figure cloaked in black garb on the opposing end of the river. Unless they dived into the rapid waters, they would be incapable of reaching the otherworldly creature. Ham could not see into the folds of the death-dealer's hood, but he expected the sight would be ghastly. A spectral hand extended from the end of one of its sleeves, pointing at the bank, and several more undead erupted from nothingness.

"We are not strong enough to fight that thing," Kildrak said. "Not yet anyway."

"Oh, I can shoots it," Beans said. "You sit back and watch me."

"Tarnation, don't get your dander up," Ham said, pulling his blunderbuss from its holster. "We ain't gonna be fighting it quite yet, especially with it on the other side of the river. 'Tis nothing but a preview of the main baddie to rile us up—get us all a-feared and whatnot, *mmhmm*."

"It's working," Nickl said.

The monsters rapidly moved forward, several reaching them this turn.

A zombie shambled to Beans and swung, slashing her across the cheek with its long, sharpened nails. She growled in response, her fiery gaze jam-packed with fury. A second trudged to Nickl's right but she ducked beneath its wild swing, twisting her dagger in preparation to strike back. More undead hobbled closer from the riverside.

Ham raised his blunderbuss thinking he would shoot the zombie by Nickl point-blank and somehow missed. He did not even know why he carried the blasted gun. He could not hit the broad side of a barn, even if he were standing inside its walls.

"Heck!" He put the gun away. On his next round, he would split their skulls the way the gods intended.

Kildrak fired twice, his first bullet striking the zombie by Beans and the second zipping over its shoulder to harmlessly ricochet off the ground on the other side.

Nickl and Beans shrieked one after the other as the enemies each landed another blow, but Ham's eyes were glued to the death-dealer weaving his hands in preparation to summon another fiend for them to face. Colored runes of magic materialized and floated in the air around the death-dealer, pulsating with energy. Ham caught his breath as a ring of fire formed about thirty feet away behind the quarter dozen monsters plodding closer.

"Well, this is going to be ugly," Kildrak said.

"I am going to need more blood leaf," Ham agreed.

A pair of skeletons reached Beans, the first striking her with a dagger. She staggered, her face paling from the blow.

"I am going to go down, muley, if you don't do something," Beans warned him, her fingers fumbling for a liquid blue at her belt. The second skeleton twisted behind her, preventing her from escaping and attacked, miraculously missing.

"Ain't nothin' gonna happen to you. Shin out from here!" Ham roared, clenching his fists. He stormed toward the first skeleton and slammed his head downward. The strike was true; bits of bony fragments exploding in every direction. Ham stepped through the wrecked remains and shoved the second skeleton back several feet, stepping into its space to protect the golden-haired gnome.

Beans threw a potion back and closed her eyes as it stitched her wounds. The zombie in front of her raised an arm to attack. Ham used his Intercept ability to smash the zombie's face inward but missed, his hoof getting tangled in the dead skeleton behind him. The zombie tore into Beans, stealing any effects the liquid blue might have had on her hit points.

"Tarnation!" Ham yelled.

Nickl's daggers carved into the zombie opposing her, plunging into his skull and splitting its misshapen head in two. The monster dropped and another took its place.

Another slug cracked loudly from Kildrak's boomstick, missing everything but the wind. He dropped to a knee to reload the weapon.

The two remaining zombies missed Nickl and Beans, yet Ham's sigh of relief was short-lived as an unearthly wail erupted from the circle of hellfire brightening at the river's edge. From the flames emerged a zombie-like creature, standing as tall as Ham, dressed in silver armor from his pauldrons to his greaves. He snarled and strode forward, carrying a smoking blunderbuss in one hand and a massive axe in his other.

As the summoning circle fizzled from existence, Ham noticed the death-dealer turn away from the battle and retreat into the forest. "I reckon this new bastard is our first boss creature, *mmhmm.*"

He heard Nickl gulp on the other side of Beans.

Ham headbutted at the elusive zombie in front of the gunslinging gnome at his hip twice and missed. Gritting his teeth, he heard Nickl screech with frustration as she missed the zombie in front of her too. Beans dropped her rifle and pulled out two pistols to kill her attacker, but the bullets flew by on either side without even coming close.

"I got them!" Kildrak shouted, firing his freshly loaded rifle two more times. His shots were also off mark.

"What in damn hell is happening? Are they invisible?" Ham snorted.

The zombie in front of Beans swung at her once more, and again Ham attempted to interrupt the attack by striking the undead first. This time his attack was successful, smashing his skull against the decaying face and staggering the monster back.

"Nice job, muley," Beans managed as Kildrak reloaded his guns again. "We won't give it another chance to strike."

Nickl dodged another attack from the zombie at her front. At the same time, the armored undead trudged closer and fired his blunderbuss over their heads.

"He will be here next round," Beans struggled to say, her life hanging on by a thread.

Ham crossed over in front of Beans to shield her from another assault, positioning himself so he was adjacent to the zombie attacking Nickl too. With two quick hits, he defeated the injured zombie and turned to face the lesser fiend.

"Take another liquid blue, *mmhmm*," Ham said to Beans.

Unwilling to use another potion from their inventory, Beans ignored Ham and raised her two black-eyed Susans to fire. One bullet ripped through the zombie's flesh, followed by two more shots from Kildrak's pepperbox rifle. The zombie wailed and fell away from Nickl.

"Now we're shooting," Ham said. Dead-faced, the boss came near enough for Ham to see the undead creature's ugly features. In its dented armor, the ghastly brute bore a resemblance to a run-over skinned cat shoved in an old-fashioned can of pork 'n' beans. "I'll be a dirty blue dick!" Ham scrunched up his face with disgust, his stomach churning at the sight. "You look to have been rode hard and put up wet, *mmhmm!*"

Meeting him eye to eye, the boss swung his axe at Ham's head, which he easily ducked beneath. The yellow-bellied cur then raised the blunderbuss to shoot Ham at point-blank range, but Ham spun sideways, the explosion of the gun ringing in his ears. He was surprised when the boss swung the axe another time and missed him by a long shot.

Nickl tumbled across the ground to gain an advantage behind the beast. "Let's get stabby!" she cried, jabbing her daggers into a break between the armor at the back of the knees.

With the ringing in his ears, Ham scarcely heard the monster screech in pain. The two marksman shots from Beans did not go unnoticed, each bullet rattling the beast's bone cage despite the armor.

Feeling bolstered by the sudden shift of the battle, Ham lifted his chin. "My name is Hamrogeni Herdstomper, but you can call me Ham." He grabbed the monster by the armor and jerked him forward, his hardened skull smashing the face inward with an acute strike. He headbutted the boss again for good measure and then tossed him backward.

The double shot of Kildrak's rifle ripped through his body as he fell to the ground, even though Ham was certain the entity was already dead.

"If that is the best the death-dealer has to offer," Ham smirked cockily, "he is gonna be in a world of hurt."

Beans ignored Ham, eyes widening at the smoking blunderbuss, seemingly forgetting her injuries. "I am taking its gun."

6

The Outer Door

Ham kicked at the dirt, taking a gander at the gigantic closed doors leading into Braewood Keep. The black square towers on either side matched the chipped stone decorating the entryway bespeaking of the sheer size of the enclosed fortress. From where he stood, the top was He guessed there to be four or five levels above ground and the gods only knew how many beneath the surface. If they had a grappling hook and some rope, they might be able to scale up to the ramparts; although, the effort would be in vain if the doors leading into the towers were locked too.

"Do you think it is full of undead?" Nickl asked from beneath his elbow. She wrung her hands together, her face etched in a fearful expression.

"*Mmhmm,*" Ham replied.

"As long as we can rest for a bit," Kildrak said from the back. "My feet are aching something terrible. I could go for a good foot rub."

"No one is touching your feet." Nickl snickered.

"Why are we here if we do not have a key?" Beans twirled the smoking blunderbuss she had picked up from the ghastly brute in her hand. She had recouped from the injuries amassed during the previous fight. Ham was surprised how easily she shook off the fact that she had nearly bit the dirt. "Shouldn't we be tracking the death-dealer to find the key to this place?"

"There has to be a way inside." Ham stepped pass Beans and pounded the door with his fist in frustration. A loud *thud* echoed inside, the iron ring handles bouncing against the wood as the door rattled. "Nickl, can you pick the lock?"

Nickl scrunched her nose, squeezing between him and the door to examine the lock. After a moment, she pulled a rolled skin from her pack and retrieved some thin pieces of iron, and then began to fiddle with the lock. After a few moments, she harrumphed. "I cannot get it open, but I do not see any traps." She wrapped her tools up and put them back in her inventory as quick as she had pulled them out. "I don't understand. No way we could have gotten this far if we could not get inside the keep."

Ham nodded. "It makes no sense. We defeated the first boss. Are we sure we searched his body all the way? He should have had a key."

"We searched him," Nickl said.

Kildrak tugged at his black beard. "Well, I suppose that would have been too easy."

"Hobble your lip, Kildrak. We are low level. That is how it is done," Ham snapped back. He scratched the back of his skull in thought, trying to calm his emotions. He needed to think about their situation in a different way. "I reckon we never needed a key at all. I reckon it was a way to give us some extra chips and experience before getting here, or even come head to head with that armored baddie." Ham swelled his chest, nodding his head in thought. "You know, I reckon I could bust through this door."

Kildrak hummed loudly and then said, "I don't think that is a good idea. It looks like solid wood."

Beans squealed in delight over him. "Oh, smash through it, muley!"

Ham grunted, almost trampling over Kildrak while trying to get past him. "Oh, I am going to. You can bet your chips, I am going to, *mmhmm*."

He stamped up the path to get a running start. Kildrak hustled into the grass behind him, gripping his rifle in his hand. Beans followed with a small cheer, jutting her hand above her head.

Nickl grinned from ear to ear, following their companions. "This is going to be awesome!"

Grabbing a packet of blood leaf from his pocket, Ham inhaled the powder into his oversized nostrils. His mind immediately buzzed with the drug filtering into his bloodstream. He rocked his head back and forth and stomped his hoof into the dirt. He was going to shatter the door into firewood!

With a low rumble, he charged forward, his friends a blur, and threw his weight, headlong, into the double doors.

The definite clunk banged inside his skull, a ring chiming in his triangular ears.

Stars dotted his vision as an impinging blackness stole away his surroundings. He bounced back and skidded onto his haunches, reaching wildly for the solid ground to steady himself and keep from falling over. "Hellfire..." he managed to wheeze.

He heard Kildrak clear his throat before declaring, "Well, we should probably try to use our heads in another way. How about we check the perimeter and see if we can find any clues or secret entrances? If we cannot find a way inside, we can always go to the next town and see what else Mister Sammich has to offer for quests. We might have come here too soon."

Ham breathed in, catching his breath and let the world come back into view. He wanted to argue with the dwarf, but nothing worth saying came to mind.

Nickl suddenly was at his side, patting him on the shoulder. "I really thought that was going to work. Are you going to be okay?"

He grumbled under his breath. "Give me a few and I'll be right as rain."

She patted him again and then skipped off. He listened to her and Bean's footsteps fade away in either direction as they worked their way along the walls of Braewood Keep, searching the stones behind the shrubs and trees.

After a short while, Kildrak followed Beans.

Once his vision cleared, Ham brought up his stat sheet, feeling pain from his forehead to the base of his neck. Sure enough, he had taken damage from throwing himself into the doors. Yet his waning alignment is what caught his eye as he slumped over his knees. He was not sure how long he sat there staring at the numbers, shaking his head in despair. If he was not careful, he would end up as wretched inside as the death-dealer.

Ham's stomach rumbled indicating it was near time to eat supper when Nickl's squeal of excitement cut through the air. "I found something! I found something!" Her little feet scurried over grass back to Ham. He scarcely saw the piece of worn parchment she waved over her head.

"Oh no." Ham groaned, throwing his head back at the sight of the paper. "I know where this is going. The *thinking* part of the adventure. Is it written in another language? Does it lead to some hidden treasure box with some puzzle we have to unravel? Or is it a note from a mysterious stranger leading us back the way we came?"

Footsteps thudded behind him, signaling the return of Kildrak and Beans.

"What did you find?" Beans asked.

Nickl smiled sweetly at Ham, fanning the paper in his face. "I don't know yet. It was shoved in a crack in the stone. I thought we could look at it together."

"Well, go ahead," Kildrak folded his arms and said, "let's have it."

Nickl did not lose her wide grin, holding the parchment out in front of her as she read it out loud.

Lay your enemies to eternal sleep,

A key I am to enter Braewood Keep,

I scream so loud; I have a nasty bite,

If you hear my roar, you're still in the fight.

"Tarnation! Just what we need—a riddle that doesn't make a lick of sense," Ham said. "This one is for y'all to figure out. I reckon I have never been too good with words, *mmhmm.*"

"It is clearly hinting at what the key is to get inside," Nickl replied, "and, by the sound of it, the key is not a *key* at all."

"But what does it mean?" Kildrak stood his rifle on end and leaned against it.

"Lots of wolves out here that have a nasty bite," Beans said. "I bet the key is tied up in the fur of some dire wolf in a hidden den nearby."

"That accounts for one part of the riddle, but not most of it." Kildrak tugged at his beard. "I think it is one of the undead. Everything we have done has surrounded the dead. We should have brought the remains of the boss. I wager that is what it is referring to."

"What?" Ham scrunched his nose.

"Eternal sleep. Nasty bite. A roar. A fight." Kildrak bobbed his head up and down, looking back the way they had come. "What other zombie or skeleton have we crossed that would be important enough to gain us entry to Braewood Keep?"

"What the horseshit?" Ham gaped at the dwarf. "I'm sure as a gun that spanking some rotten carcass against the door ain't gonna get us inside. You've dang near gone coon, *mmhmm.*"

"I sure hope that isn't it. It will take us two weeks to retrieve the corpse and make it back here again," Beans said, "and that is only if its body is still there. Probably dragged off by wolves...you sure it is not talking about a wolf?"

"I-I don't think it's the undead or wolves," Nickl said. "The guards at Toonok Tower were supposed to have the key before it was taken. They would not be keeping a monster or an animal with them. Ham—" Nickl scratched her head in thought, "repeat what you said again."

"What?" Ham scoffed. "That Kildrak is off his nut."

"No. You said something about *a gun.*"

"I said I'm sure as a gun that spanking—"

"A gun," Beans echoed. "You're a genius, Nickl. It is a gun! The key is a gun."

Ham jerked his blunderbuss loose and examined it. "No gun is going to fit inside that itty-bitty keyhole."

"I bet we have to shoots it!" Beans flashed her pearly whites.

"Makes sense to me, *mmhmm*." Ham pointed the end of his barrel at the double doors. "We are packing enough iron to blast the door to smithereens. Should we all shoot together." He twisted his neck to look at Kildrak. "C'mon, get that pepperbox up and get ready to fire, Kildrak."

"You think we are supposed to shoot the door?" Kildrak pinched his eyebrows, and then waggled his mustache. "I mean, really?"

Beans dropped the smoking blunderbuss to her feet and pulled her twin-barreled shotgun off her back. "Last one to shoots it has to rub Kildrak's feet."

"Ha! I like the sound of that." Kildrak laughed.

The crack and boom of Ham's blunderbuss and Bean's shotgun resounded repeatedly. Even Nickl cried out in desperation, covering one ear and yanking a six-shooter from Bean's belt to shoot at the door. After the barrels were empty and the smoke cleared, Ham moved closer to inspect the wood. He rubbed his fingers along the smooth wood.

"What in tarnation?" Ham's jaw dropped. "I don't even see a scratch on the door."

"How is that possible?" Beans shouted.

Nickl carefully slipped Bean's gun back in its holster. "Before you started shooting, I was going to suggest you try that one." She pointed the smoking blunderbuss on the ground.

"Ah," Ham rubbed his chin, "I reckon we should try the magical-looking gun."

Beans scooped it up with a laugh and fired at the door. Ham was not surprised when the door swung open, though he noticed Kildrak's beard drop against his chest in surprise.

Nickl clapped her hands in delight.

"I would have never thought shooting the door would have opened it," Kildrak remarked.

Beans smiled blowing the smoke off the edge of the gun. "We have made it. I am fairly sure I just leveled up."

"Me too. I think we all did," Ham said. "I guess we had the key after all, *mmhmm*."

"Now there is matter of who is rubbing my feet," Kildrak said. "By my calculation, I believe Nickl was the last one to shoot?"

Nickl scrunched her face and stuck out her tongue. "Your *calculations* are wrong. You didn't even shoot a gun. You're rubbing your own feet."

7

Braewood Keep

DAY 175, 4023 CE

Iron slugs rampaged down the stone hallway like sideways rain, ricocheting off walls and blasting through the undead lumbering toward them. Ham fought to see beyond the rotting corpses and skeletal hands reaching for them. He suspected two dozen were squeezed up in the tight space, but he was never too good at counting.

"Reloading!" Kildrak bellowed as the last round fired from the end of his rifle. Ham heaved against the leading zombie, shoving him into the rest and stalling the enemy's advance. The dwarf grumbled behind him. "There are too many. Why are we even here?"

Ham rumbled in his throat while considering the question. He was not sure how to explain how investigating a pestilence on a farm had somehow led them to tracking down a death-dealer halfway across Squall's End. He honestly was not sure it made any sense, nor was he certain it needed an explanation. They were champions and were known to live a bizarre lifestyle. In fact, by definition, nothing about their lives was regular.

"Chips and experience," Ham uttered, blasting his blunderbuss at the horde. A ghastly head near the front snapped back. He gave a wry grin, saying softer, "Chips and experience, *mmhmm*."

Beans whooped with excitement in front of him. "And to shoots *things*!"

"We could gain another level before reaching the top of this cotton-picking place." Ham held his smile and rubbed his nose. The itch for another hit of bloodleaf tickled his senses. "I tell you what, when we are done with that death-dealer, he is gonna be as cold as a wagon tire."

"You got that right, muley." Beans beamed, firing her smoking gun in front of him. The horde stumbled back again. Deathly moans and groans echoed from hidden passageways farther back.

"Must be a million of them," Nickl said from under Ham's elbow.

Kildrak lifted his weapon to fire again. "I don't think there are that many."

Nickl tapped her chin in thought and then reached inside of her pocket. "Should I throw a bomb?"

"No!" Kildrak frantically cried. "We are in a narrow pass with several floors of stone above us. An explosion would bury us!"

Ham snorted. "Tarnation, Kildrak. Don't be puttin' that out in the universe for the gods to be hearing unless you want them to crush us where we stand. Did you learn nothing from your naysaying at Toonok Tower?"

"The guards showing up in an airship was not my fault," Kildrak said.

"This tower is not going to fall." Beans waved him off. "Throw the bomb, Nickl."

As much as I hate to admit it, Kildrak is right," Ham said. "We cannot risk being crushed under rubble. But we have been standing around too long. I am tired of fighting these bastards."

Nickl pulled her fist from her pocket, empty-handed. "What do we do, then?"

Ham snorted, rolling his shoulders back. "I am going to bash some skulls while y'all keep shooting."

"What?" Nickl widened her eyes.

Ham did not wait to explain, stamping his hoof against the ground and barrelling forward. He roared, lowering his head and smashing through the zombies and skeletons. Bodies lurched in all directions as he ploughed through them. Gunshots boomed on either side of him as Kildrak and Beans unloaded their weapons on the disoriented undead.

Ham staggered, slamming his skull down into the closest skeleton and bursting its skull. He heard Nickl's daggers scraping against bone as she followed him, cutting into anything that stirred in his wake.

"Last one!" Beans shouted, flipping her gun upward and shooting a final zombie struggling to stand ahead of Ham. The bullet pierced the skull and dropped it on its fellow undead.

"I reckon that takes care of that, *mmhmm*." Ham snickered, wiping the remains of the undead from his brow. He huffed, surprised he did not take any damage from the wild act. He stepped over the pile of dead. The sound of additional undead that had been coming up the funnel faded in the opposite direction. "Looks like we can rest for a spell. The enemy skedaddled back into their hidey hole."

"Gosh, that was brave." Nickl smacked Ham on the back of his thigh. Her eyes trailed his own down the corridor. "I hope they stay gone for a while. We have been swinging and shooting since we made it inside."

Kildrak neared Ham's side, slinging his gun over his shoulder. "Why would they run? They are mindless undead. Your wild antics shouldn't frighten them in the slightest."

"Who cares?" Beans wriggled between them with a grunt, looking at the scattered remains at their feet. "Look at all these bodies we can loot."

"They cannot have much on them. They were barely wearing clothes," Kildrak said.

"No harm in looking, is there?" Beans said.

Kildrak frowned at the gnome. "I won't stand in your way."

"I, on the other hand, am gonna make hay while the sun shines and let you get to your rummaging, *mmhmm*," Ham said, pulling out another dose of bloodleaf. He turned it over in his fingers with a smile and made his way to the edge of the corridor to keep watch. He knew if he was not careful, he would run out of the drug before making it to the top of the tower, but a little more right now would not hurt.

Behind him, he heard Beans and Nickl rifling through the corpses. Looking over his shoulder, he noticed Kildrak watching the other side from whence they had come, combing his beard with his fingers. Seeing nothing to be concerned over, Ham snorted the drug and leaned back against the wall. He closed his eyes, basking in the moment as the powdery substance enhanced his senses and hardened his muscles. He suspected he could dang near stomp through another hundred undead before tiring.

Before long, he heard Beans laugh manically with delight. "Look at the size of this gem," she cried out, lifting a blue jewel above her head. "I bet I could trade this for a new gun when we get back to Mister Sammich. Maybe even two guns. It has to be worth a fortune."

"Oh! Where did you find that?" Nickl asked, her tone dripping with jealousy. She scooted away from the body she had been examining and gawked at the blue gem.

Beans pointed at a dead zombie at her feet. "It was in the pocket of his britches."

Nickl stomped her foot somewhat playfully. "No fair! I was just looking over there. I can't believe I—"

Ham's eyes bulged as Nickl was cut off by Beans's pained scream, the merriment stripped from her mien. The gem glowed brightly before magically melting between her fingers, swiftly forging a blue iron gauntlet over her hand.

"What is happening?" Kildrak left his post, shouting over Beans. He instinctively pulled the butt of his gun to his shoulder and aimed at her hand. "What is that?"

"I don't know," Ham said, nearing with caution.

Nickl scurried away from Beans, ducking behind Ham. "I don't want it anymore."

"Oh, it—it hurts." Beans stifled her moan, grabbing the glimmering gauntlet with her free hand. She jerked it with all her strength, her eyes watering in desperation. The metal glove did not budge. She released it with a belated whine. "I cannot get it off. I cannot move my hand. I—I can't shoots my gun like this."

"Oh no..." Nickl gasped.

As though trying to prove her point, she lifted the smoking blunderbuss and tried to fit the gauntlet finger around the trigger. Then, despairingly, she moved the gun to rest on the gauntlet so she could pull the trigger with her left hand. "This is going to increase my miss chance."

"Let's not start fussin' until we have a look-see, *mmhmm*," Ham said, reaching for the gauntlet with his meaty hand. "I bet I can yank this thing right off."

"And her arm with it," Kildrak muttered.

"Ah, shut your pie hole," Ham said. "I'll be careful."

Kildrak hurried to grab Ham's arm before he had a chance to touch the gauntlet. "It is cursed, Ham. I would not fiddle with it until we find a way to remove it safely."

Beans cried out again in pain, falling back on her buttocks. "Ow. Ow. Ow."

"We need to get her back to town!" Nickl screeched. "Find a healer or something."

"There is no time." Beans scrunched up her face and swiped her stat sheet so it was visible to them. "It...it is sapping my life. It...it is killing me."

BEANS			LEVEL 3	3925/6000
MEDIUM	GNOME	GUN ENTHUSIAST	CHAOTIC EVIL	'40
POWER	6		HP	12/25
DEXERTITY	14		ARMOR	9
ENDURANCE	8			
INTELLIGENCE	16		SKILLS	SPELLS
AWARENESS	10		PERCEPTION	-
CHARISMA	12		SHARPSHOOTER	-
LUCK	6		HISTORY	
DEFECT	STEALING		CHIPS	480

Her face noticeably paled, the numbers rapidly falling from her hit points.

"Hang tight. I am going to pull it free." Ham pushed the dwarf to the side.

"And what happens when you pull it free and it affixes itself to you instead," Kildrak snapped at Ham. "Are you going to let it drain your life instead? Will you die for her?"

Ham froze, feeling Nickl hovering behind him. He was getting closer with every moment to becoming an NPC. If he were to let himself bite the ground, he would have to incarnate all over again and start his quest over. Everything he had done up until now would be completely pointless.

He gulped and looked at Nickl. He would be abandoning his closest friend.

"We cannot just let her die," Nickl said in a soft voice, holding onto Ham. She seemed afraid to lose him too. "We can give her liquid blue to keep her alive until we find a solution."

"How many do we have?" Ham asked. Beans wailed again, holding her little fist against her chest.

Kildrak tugged at his beard. "Two. At this rate, she won't even make it out of Braewood, let alone travel the distance to the nearest town."

"Tarnation!"

Beans coughed weakly, laying her head back on the ground. "It...it is okay. I will come find you again after I reincarnate. I will ask Mister Sammich where to find you. You...you cannot waste your liquid blue on me."

"You will be too low level to join our party again," Nickl said. "Besides, you probably won't remember anything."

The gnome girl winced, her final words a whisper. "I will...remember."

Beans's body went limp, the smoking blunderbuss rolling from her grasp and the gauntlet turning back to a blue gem in her lifeless palm.

"No!" Ham roared. "How could we have let her die by a damn stone? We should have done something more."

Nickl pulled Ham back as though he might touch the stone.

"We had no choice." Kildrak's voice quivered. He knelt and picked up the magical gun to add to those he already carried. "That was a nasty item to have hidden here. We might be too low level to be traipsing these halls."

"Where else should we be?" Nickl asked.

"Nowhere else. This is where we were supposed to go." Ham ran his thick fingers across his head, fearful of knowing how his decision to let her die impacted his already failing alignment. He pulled at his stumped horns while staring at Beans's corpse, repeating himself. "But we should have done something more..."

For a moment, they stood there together in dismay. When Nickl finally spoke, Ham nearly jumped out of his skin. "We need to keep going, but should we say some words...about her?"

Ham bobbed his chin. "I never been too good with words, I reckon, but I will say, she had sand. She had a lot of sand, that's fer shore."

8

Hopeless

Ham's chest heaved, hearing the quick footsteps of the undead chasing them down the hallway. He straggled behind Nickl and Kildrak through the winding corridor, looking for a room in which to hide. For a moment, he glanced over his shoulder at the ghouls; their animalistic movements contrasted with the lifelessness in their eyes as they bounded off the walls in a swarm.

"This way!" Kildrak bellowed, drawing Ham's attention forward. The dwarf took a hard left through a narrow doorframe. Nickl squealed and skittered behind him in her desperate attempt to get away from the looming undead at Ham's heel.

Ham followed her, spinning into the room and slamming the door shut in a fluid motion. He braced his shoulders against the door. The undead smashed into the opposite side, scraping and screeching in their attempt to tear through the thick wood.

"I hate this darned place!" Ham growled, hurriedly glancing around the small room. A singular window was on the opposite wall, the waning light of dusk piercing into the dismal chamber. Rotted barrels and debris of age-old wares littered the floor and lone table that Nickl had somehow stooped beneath upon entering. Her thin arms wrapped tightly around a wooden leg, her shoulders rising and falling rapidly while trying to catch her breath. She averted her gaze as Ham reached for a dose of blood leaf. His thick fingers trembled as he thumbed through the few remaining packets.

"Do you have enough to defeat the death-dealer?" Nickl pushed herself up from the floor, scooted to Ham's side, and raised herself up on her tippy toes. She investigated the pouch on his belt. "You don't have much left, Ham."

"There is never enough," he quavered before gently redirecting her with his hand and lifting the powder to his nose. He took a deep huff.

Her face scrunched up with concern, her eyes lingering where his hand had brushed her aside. "How much have you been taking?"

Ham frowned. He considered Nickl and blinked a couple times. He heard her question along with a ringing between his ears, having no answer to give her.

Kildrak lay his pepperbox rifle down on the table, and the clanging pulled Nickl's attention from Ham. The dwarf crossed his arms at the two of them. "I told you we are too low level to be in this miserable keep. If the death-dealer is at the top, he will cut us down. We should travel back to Mister Sammich and find something to give us a bit more experience and then return."

"Ham can beat the death-dealer!" Nickl waved her finger in the air. "Beans may not be with us anymore, but we can win. We have two liquid blues left and...and *some* blood leaf. If we defeat the undead out there, we might even level up again."

"We have to complete the quest," Kildrak agreed, "but we cannot win this fight. The undead would rip us to shreds."

"He is one floor up. We are so close!"

Ham tried to ignore the wails behind him. His thoughts were scattered and although he knew he had enough, his fingers were already inching for another parcel of blood leaf. "We don't know he is up there. It is probably another boss with another clue to another location, *mmhmm*." The door rattled at his back. "We defeated the last boss without breaking a sweat. I reckon we could do it again."

"Why risk it? Nothing is stopping us from returning." Kildrak pointed at the smoking blunderbuss. "We have the key."

Ham clenched his fist above his pouch and then smacked the door behind him. "I have no intention of turning tail, dwarf. We are four floors off the ground with no escape, and there are more undead out there than whiskers on your chin. I'll be damned if I came all this way to watch Beans die and then run away."

"And I did not come all this way to die." He turned away from Ham, gesturing to the floor under the paneless window. "We have a rope and a grappling hook right here. I say we make our escape."

Ham followed his finger. "That rope won't hold us. Who knows how long it has been laying here in this dump, *mmhmm*."

"We have a better chance with the rope than fighting the

undead. We might even find another champion to join us on this quest."

"You want to replace Beans?" Nickl stomped at the ground. "She has barely been gone a couple of hours."

"Bah!" Kildrak harrumphed. "She isn't dead-dead. She is reincarnated in a tavern somewhere, probably already on her first adventure with another adventuring group. You do not have to mourn over her."

Nickl's jaw dropped, stepping from Kildrak. "I will mourn her, thank you very much."

"I am not being cruel. We are champions. We live. We die. We live again."

"You are barkin' at a knot, dwarf!" The ruckus behind the door intensified. Ham clenched his teeth and slammed his fist into the wood again. "She may be dead and alive again, but the decisions we made about not trying to save her cost us. Look here."

Ham wanted to shut his eyes as he revealed his stat sheet, but his guilt would not allow it. While he could ignore Nickl's and Kildrak's shaken expressions, he was incapable of unhearing their gasps, which were loud enough to surpass the din outside the room.

Due to choosing his own livelihood over Beans—in addition to his other poor choices since incarnating—Ham's alignment score continued to plummet. According to the new numbers, his mind shifted from a place of good-hearted intentions to a realm of evil thinking. Even now, images of violence and wickedness flooded his mind, softened only by the drugs coursing in his veins. Then again, the blood leaf was its own temptation to consider, one which he did not have the focus or interest to mull over right now.

HAMROGENI "HAM" HERDSTOMPER			LEVEL 3	3905/6000
MEDIUM	MINOTAUR	BARBARIAN	NEUTRAL EVIL	'44
POWER	16		HP	30/33
DEXERTITY	14		ARMOR	12
ENDURANCE	14			
INTELLIGENCE	6		SKILLS	SPELLS
AWARENESS	8		INTIMIDATE	IDENTIFY
CHARISMA	4		SURVIVAL	MARKSMAN
LUCK	2		SEAFARING	
			INTERCEPT	
DEFECT	BLOOD LEAF ADDICTION		CHIPS	345

"Your insides are turning rotten," Kildrak said. The dwarf's pudgy fingers inched onto the flat surface of the table, stopping near the smoking blunderbuss. "You need to go do some charity work, or donate to one of the churches, or something."

"Tarnation! I ain't doing nothing of the sort." His alignment ticked down another number and he hurried to swipe away his stat sheet with hopes that no one noticed. Nickl's paled face suggested she had indeed caught sight of the slight adjustment. Ham rambled to keep her from saying anything about it. "As soon as I bust the skull of whatever beast is awaiting above us, I will be spending my chips on some good ol' blood leaf, *mmhmm*. Sure as a gun that bone-bag chump will need charity when I am done with him."

He bulled his blunderbuss free from its holster. He would rip through every one of the undead like Nickl suggested and level again before fighting whatever awaited him upstairs.

"H-Ham?" Nickl stammered.

"Let's fill 'em full of lead."

"Ham! No!" Kildrak cried out as Ham jerked around and flung the door open.

The undead on the other side, spoiled skin and muscle peeling from the bone, attempted to flood through the opening. Ham connected head-on, muscle against their mass, doing his best to use his body as a barricade. They slammed into him, nearly pushing him into the chamber before realizing they would have to rip through him first.

Ham fired the gun, blowing the brains out of the leading zombie, and then headbutted the second. It staggered back for a moment and then lurched at Ham.

Clawed hands raked the air in front of him, inches from his snout. The mishmash of skeletons and zombies on either side took their turn with no better result. *Tarnation.* He could not believe his luck! Using his body to block the creatures from barreling through to Kildrak and Nickl, Ham pressed into them and struggled to dodge more wild attacks. Two more clawed hands missed him entirely, but a third gaunt hand reached out from the horde and ripped across his chest.

Ham fought through the pain, his eyes avoiding the crimson liquid seeping from his flesh and into his chest hair. The nails might as well have been knives. With a low growl, he flung his head into the closest rotting corpse. His horn stump grazed a skull, doing little, if any, damage.

Kildrak's gun boomed, the bullets zipping by Ham's head into the mass of undead. "This is suicide. We need to run!"

Ham ignored him, swatting away the feeble attempts of several more undead swinging at him. He could not count how many were piled down the hall, pushing and scrambling over one another to get to him. With a mad grin, he head-butted the closest one, shattering its skull.

"You are going to get yourself killed," Nickl shouted from his side as he reloaded the blunderbuss. She reached her arm around him to stab at a skeleton with her dagger and missed.

Ham flared his nostrils. His temples pulsated from the drugs in his system. "I ain't no yellow-belly. Not gonna see me shin out!"

Beans wouldn't run away.

He heard Kildrak's dissatisfied grumbling as he fired at the swarm of undead. The bullet was inches from Ham, tearing through the chest of another zombie. Gurgles and hisses rose up from the horde in response, their combined weight pushing against him once more.

He fired the blunderbuss, the shrapnel ripping through the zombies in front, tearing them in half. And still the bastards came at him ravenously. With a forced roar, Ham stooped his shoulders and shoved back, the muscles in his arms and back feeling like they might split in two with the effort. Their fingers and teeth scraped against at his exposed flesh, as though they would strip him to the bone then and there. His cry became a high-pitched whine, the breath flee-ing his lungs; to his shock, his hooves started to scoot back across the floor.

"Ham!"

Nickl's scream was drowned out by the cacophony of the undead.

"We are getting out of here!" Kildrak shouted all the louder, his footsteps retreating from the doorway.

From the corner of his eye, the gleaming iron of Nickl's

knives flashed as she carved at the undead fanning out into the room. The clinking of metal on stone sounded behind him, suggesting Kildrak was securing the grappling hook on the window.

"Go with him," Ham directed. Blood dribbled into his eye from a cut somewhere on his brow. In desperation, Ham awkwardly tried to connect his skull into another undead and whiffed, almost losing his balance.

"I will not leave you here," Nickl shouted. Kildrak grunted behind them as he hoisted himself through the window. "If you want to die here, then I will start over with you! We are together until the end, Hamrogeni Herdstomper."

He held his jaw firmly in response to his friend's proclamation. The undead struck him multiple times, dropping his hit points to almost zero. He could not see her die too, especially after they had come so far. Through clenched teeth, he said, "I will follow after you. I promise."

Nickl bobbed her head with excitement and skittered off to the window. Soon after, he heard her call to him. "Come on, Ham. You promised."

With a mighty push, Ham withdrew from the horde and leaped to the window, tangling his fingers around the rope in the nick of time. His large build barely fit through the frame, coming close to crushing Nickl against the stone wall on the other side. Heaving himself downward, Ham caught a glimpse of Kildrak scooting toward the bottom as quick as his stubby legs could move him down the wall.

The undead above him screeched, several leaping out the window.

"Hang on!" Ham shouted, moving sideways and pulling

the rope with him. Kildrak and Nickl gave surprised shouts as they were pulled from their positions below and shifted sideways along the wall. Several skeletons and zombies spiraled by them, the bodies exploding against the ground upon impact.

Ham looked skyward to ensure no more undead were following when he caught the shape of a dark figure, the death-dealer, peering from a window on the highest floor. A shadow fell over him and his companions, the darkness in his heart swelling against his will.

He swore he saw the shape of a smile form in the shadows beneath the hood.

Skunked

The death-dealer's grin haunted Ham.

Tossing back a shot of tarantula juice, Ham banged the glass onto the countertop and motioned to the barkeep to give him a refill. Two days of snorting blood leaf had done nothing to rid him of the image, but he suspected enough whiskey might do the trick. To his left, Kildrak twisted toward Ham, the stool squeaking underneath him. From the corner of his eye, he saw the dwarf open his mouth as though he might say something, probably about getting tangle-footed if he had too much to drink, but Ham silenced him by slamming his other fist against the wood.

The barkeep brusquely turned to Ham, raising a bottle to top him off. "Having a rough adventure, champion?" The overweight human took a breath, his fat stomach rising and falling under his tattered apron. He finished filling the glass before continuing. "I have seen that look on many adventurers, but dark times catch us all. Like any storm, it'll blow on by."

"I don't recall askin' you, barkeep." Ham grabbed the glass and downed it in a single gulp before pushing it back. "Fill the glass and keep your trap shut, *mmhmm.*"

The bulbous man snapped his lips together, narrowing his gaze at Ham while filling the drink once more. As he pulled the bottle away, he said through clenched teeth, "Consider that your last round."

Ham met the barkeep's eye and jerked at his blunderbuss in its holster. "I will be done when I say I am done, *mmhmm.*"

Kildrak grabbed Ham's knuckles, stopping his movement and keeping the gun from coming free from its holding. "Finish your drink, Ham. Nickl will be waiting for us outside soon enough anyway."

Ham scowled, looking over Kildrak to examine the tavern. He realized for the first time that Nickl was not with them. He did not remember her scampering off.

As Ham rotated back around, the barkeep commented snidely, "I should have listened to my mother. Never give advice to a hornless minotaur."

With a snort, Ham swatted away Kildrak's hand and reached for his drink again. The barkeep wandered down the counter to another patron before Ham could say anything more. He doubted the man's mother ever said anything of the sort. He glowered at the counter. "Where is she?"

"You sent her to fetch more blood leaf," Kildrak said with disdain, his seat squeaking again as he adjusted his weight. "And I asked her to speak to Mister Sammich to see what other champions were available to join us. We cannot finish our quest alone."

"You have a hankering to get them killed too?"

Kildrak's throaty growl sounded like it could have come from Ham. "We did not get anyone killed. Beans picked up a cursed item and it took her life. It happens to the best of us. You could not have done anything to stop it without killing yourself."

"Maybe I should have," Ham countered before gulping his drink down. He exposed his stat sheet to Kildrak. "I reckon those numbers say I made the wrong decision in letting her die like she did, *mmhmm.* Might be best if I start this whole adventure over again."

HAMROGENI "HAM" HERDSTOMPER			LEVEL 3	4105/6000
MEDIUM	MINOTAUR	BARBARIAN	NEUTRAL EVIL	32
POWER	16		HP	33/33
DEXERTITY	14		ARMOR	13
ENDURANCE	14			
INTELLIGENCE	6		SKILLS	SPELLS
AWARENESS	8		INTIMIDATE	IDENTIFY
CHARISMA	4		SURVIVAL	MARKSMAN
LUCK	2		SEAFARING	
			INTERCEPT	
DEFECT	BLOOD LEAF ADDICTION		CHIPS	88

The dwarf sat for a moment, examining the stat sheet including Ham's less-than-satisfactory alignment. After a long silence, he responded in a soft, almost comforting tone. "Those numbers are an accumulation of some bad decisions, but choosing to go left when you could go right does not make you wicked. I would not be fighting alongside you if you were."

"You think I am good?"

"I do."

Ham began to argue. "You're the one who said I was turning rotten inside. Doesn't sound like you have your head screwed on straight. Maybe you should go elsewhere and fight—"

"These lands are being infected by a death-dealer," Kildrak cut him off, "twisting light to dark and living to dead. Seems to me, it has had a toll on more than the landscape. I would think you are victim to its darkness too. And I suspect if we can end the death-dealer, we can set you right again."

Blinking slowly, Ham let the dwarf's words sink in. The small bastard was not good for much, but suggesting that the recent shadow setting over his mind was the result of the death-dealer and not his own foul interior undoubtedly sparked something inside him. He tried to focus on the feeling of goodness, but his thoughts peppered, a sudden wave of negativity washing over him and preventing any optimistic thoughts from fully maturing.

"Horse feathers, Kildrak. We cannot beat the death-dealer. He is too powerful. We barely got out of there by the skin of our teeth." Ham looked at his empty glass as though a hearty gaze and a willful heart would refill it. "Why don't you bend an elbow with me, *mmhmm*. We can find another rum-hole to paint our tongues in. Sure as heck we can find some better prairie dew."

"I told you I don't drink." Kildrak slid from the stool. "Do you really want Nickl and me to head back to Braewood Keep without you?"

Ham snapped his attention to Kildrak. "You will not take Nickl back there. She'll get killed."

"I am not taking Nickl anywhere. She is going because she wants to destroy the death-dealer and become an NPC again. She is tired of the adventuring life. Remember?" Kildrak tilted his head so he was looking up at Ham, his round, flat nose raised too high to be comfortable. Ham scrunched his face at the sight, seeing the dwarf's mustache hairs growing out of his wide nostrils. "I have heard you two talking about leaving the champion life. This is your chance and she is not about to pass it by."

Ham looked at his stat sheet still hovering in the air. "The only chance I have right now is to become an evil NPC or to be reincarnated."

"Kill the death-dealer then and set things right," Kildrak tried again. Ham rocked his head back and forth, scoffing at the remark. He could not see why the dwarf did not understand the hopelessness of the situation. Kildrak raised his voice. "For Nickl's sake, if you are planning on wasting your life, you can at least die trying to keep her safe as long as you can."

Upon mentioning keeping Nickl safe, a buzz in the back of his skull grew from a soft hum to the roar of an airship, nearly rattling his eyeballs. He suspected it was the whiskey causing the ruckus, but it did not change the fact that Kildrak was right. He needed to keep Nickl safe. He likely made that promise to himself at some point in his life.

"I reckon I can do that."

"Well...let's go then." Kildrak nodded, motioning for Ham to follow. They headed out the front door and into the streets, the boisterous sounds of the tavern fading behind them. Ham lifted his hand to block the sunrays burning into his eyes.

"Where in tarnation are we?"

"Fosterhold," Kildrak responded. "About five leagues south of Braewood."

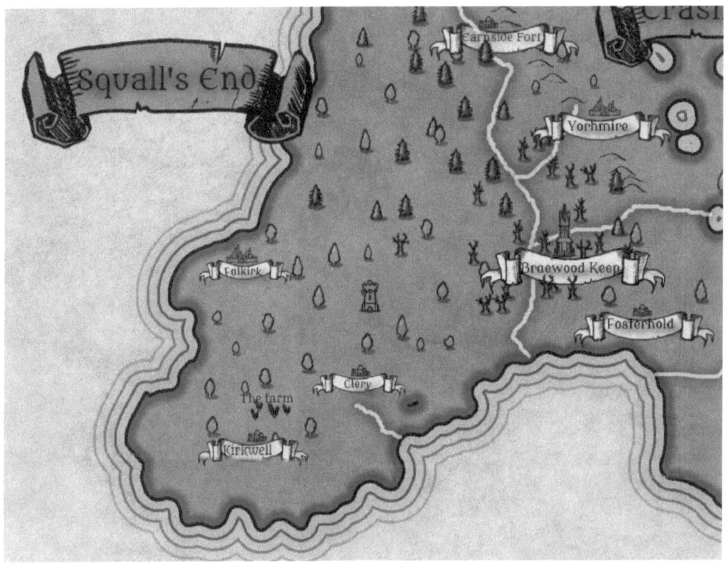

Ham squinted at the rows of buildings, catching sight of two large towers standing behind the town's border. "Never heard of it."

"We have been here for a couple of days."

"And where is Nickl?"

Kildrak twisted around in the street. "She should have been back here by now."

Shouts up the road caught Ham's attention, where guards

and a larger crowd seemed to be gathering. Through his drunken haze, it was difficult to tell what was happening exactly, but Kildrak mumbled something that sounded like *Nickl*. As the dwarf picked up his pace to investigate, Ham noticed the figure of Mister Sammich slipping away from the chaos.

"Where's he wandering off to in such a hurry?"

Kildrak did not respond, pointing to an oversized guard wearing a feathered helmet. "This is not good."

The armored guard bellowed over the crowd. "Move back, citizens. We have apprehended the criminal. Nothing more to see here until she hangs from the gallows."

"What is her crime, Captain?" a woman yelled.

"Yeah. What did she do?" a man echoed.

Several more guards without feathered helmets moved through the crowd, their iron breastplates reflecting in the sunlight as the Captain answered. "Attacking guards at Toonok Tower after crimes were imposed in Clery. Do not worry. Justice will be dealt swiftly."

"Let me go!" Nickl's shrill tone pierced the air from somewhere within the mass of people.

Ham swayed closer to the crowd, almost tripping over his own feet. He felt Kildrak's hand brush by him for a moment as he passed. He pleaded to Ham as he passed. "Don't hurt anyone!"

Pushing by Kildrak, Ham only thought of keeping Nickl safe. His hooves slammed against the sandy road harder than he intended. He shouted over the din of people. "Captain, we know this is a horse's haul of poppycock. That is Nickl Nackl of Clan Paddiwackle, a noble lass. You surely have heard of her father, *mmhmm.*"

The captain turned to Ham with a jerk, placing his hand on the hilt of his sword. The crowd divided, leaving a clear path between them. Nickl came into view, held firmly in place by two guardsmen on the opposite side of the man in armor. She looked to Ham with wide eyes as the remaining guard filed into place behind her.

Ham estimated a dozen or more.

"I know who she is and I know you, Hamro—"

"My name is Hamrogeni Herdstomper and you can call me Ham," he slurred as though the captain had asked his name instead of being halfway through saying it. He did not realize what happened until he was almost done with his spiel, chuckling to himself as he finished the sentence. He wondered how much of that tarantula juice he had swallowed.

"I know." The captain's face tensed. "Now, you will throw down your arms and hang with her."

"What?" Ham looked at his arms for a moment, flexing every muscle from his biceps to his hands. He caught sight of his blunderbuss under his elbow. "Oh, you mean my guns. Listen, I am about as full as a tick right now, and I don't want any trouble, you hear? But you cannot arrest us. If you do, the fat's really going to be in the fire, *mmhmm.*"

"What are you blathering about?"

"See, her and I are champions—"

"That does not give you the right to kill innocents!"

"—and we have a death-dealer to turn belly up."

The crowd gasped fearfully at the mention of the fiend, but the captain's face remained expressionless. He crossed his arms and took a step closer to Ham. "Death-dealer or not, you will be hanged until you are dead. We will find more honorable—principled—champions to respond to this alleged threat." The captain nodded expectantly at the gun at Ham's side. "Hand over your weapons."

"You are going to have a hard time finding anyone willing to wrestle with that pale-skinned bastard, but I s'pose I would let you stretch my neck if you let the lass go," Ham said. "She did nothing wrong."

"Her innocence will be decided by the local magistrate." He motioned to the guards behind him. "I will not tell you again."

Remembering that Kildrak had been with him a moment ago, Ham turned around to get his advice. He was not seeing much chance of getting away without busting a few skulls, but he was going to need the dwarf's firepower to get them out alive. No chance he could lick all the guards on his own with whiskey in his veins.

He was surprised to find the dwarf gone from sight. "Dang, he cut stick, didn't he?"

"Ham, it's okay!" Nickl squealed. "We can sort this out."

It took him two tries to find the gun at his side. He finally pulled it free and dropped it to the ground. "I reckon we don't have much of a choice."

10

Bad Medicine

DAY 180, 4023 CE

Ham was no closer to finding sobriety on the path to the magistrate's office than he was when sitting in the tavern with Kildrak. The buildings and people of Fosterhold blurred around him, their voices a low hum in his ears. Kicking up dirt, he trekked along behind the captain while Nickl stayed at his side, offering repeated reassurances they would sort everything out.

"We didn't do anything wrong. The magistrate will have to see that," she clamored on, rubbing her hands on her neck as though they would protect her from a rope. She looked around at the guards surrounding them. Ham struggled to stay focused on her voice. "We are not going to be hanged. This has all been a mistake."

Ham turned his chin to see raised gallows on his right, a wooden platform beneath a wooden beam with three nooses hanging toward the dirt. Nickl seemed to do all she could to avoid the sight, darting her eyes down the road. He grumbled, shifting his attention to a square building ahead. Its columned entry and brass door marked it as a domicile for governance. He tensed his jaw. "You sure ain't done a thing, but I have done plenty. We will make sure this lawman understands the truth of it."

He felt Nickl's hand rest on his elbow. "Don't talk like that. We have all slipped up a bit, but you are a good champion." She bobbed her head. "And a good friend."

"You two save your talk for the magistrate," the captain said without emotion, signaling to the guards ahead to open the singular door to the establishment.

Ham squinted at the back of the captain's head, Nickl's words rattling between his ears. He wondered what she saw that he could not. He did not feel like he was a *good* anything.

The thick door swung open. The captain led the way inside with Ham and Nickl filing in behind him. A couple guards followed too, while the majority remained outside the building knowing there would not be enough room inside. Ham joined the rest in an open foyer. A corridor to a study was straight ahead with a couple closed doors on either side of the hall. Within eyesight, behind a mahogany desk, sat the magistrate wearing a feathered hat and silken clothes. He did not lift his head, scribbling frantically on a piece of parchment with a quilled pen.

"Always bursting through my door when I am busy. No one in this town has any respect for the working man," he muttered under his breath. He did not bother lifting his head, barking at them, "What do you want?"

"Magistrate Cheddar, we seized two of the criminals who committed wrongdoings in Clery and at Toonok

Tower—Hamrogeni Herdstomper and Nickl Nackl." The captain approached the desk, the guards following behind Ham and Nickl, directing them to follow. "You may remember their wanted posters coming across your desk earlier this week. If you can sentence them, we will get the hanging underway."

"You think you are funny coming in here and insulting me, brother." Magistrate Cheddar sneered at this desk, pausing mid-scribble. With a final snort, he scratched his signature onto the paper and threw down his pen.

The captain chuckled. "Cheddar always had a better ring to it than Charlie."

"You have no right. I am the authority here. You are not allowed to come in here and tell me how to do my job, Adam!" With gritted teeth, Charlie raised his gaze. His face scrunched for a moment as though he smelled something unpleasant. He briefly shook his head at Ham before settling back on the captain.

"Run to Father if you have a problem with it," the captain remarked. "Now, pass judgment so I can—"

"Were there not more so-called champions responsible for the crimes? Kildrak Torunn and—"

"They will come to justice soon enough," The captain barked over him. "Right now, we have these two in our custody and their fate waiting outside at the gallows."

"We didn't do anything wrong!" Nickl squealed at the mention of the hanging nooses, her tone weakening with the second half of her protest. "At least, not intentionally. We have honestly done more good than not."

The magistrate eyed Nickl, his eyes widening at her sudden outburst.

"Y'all are gettin' ahead of yourselves, trying to squat with your spurs on, *mmhmm*," Ham bellowed right after her. He twisted his neck to look at the captain and magistrate. They damn near could have been twins; in fact, they most likely were. He stomped his hoof. "You want to punish me for my evil ways, I won't complain none. My insides are 'bout as rotten as a swamp hag's undercarriage. But this lass here, and the others, had no part in any offense regarding your laws or scripture books or whatever the hell writings you need to part right from wrong. So dab that ink stick with your fancy letters and hemp me up if need be, but you will leave the rest alone."

The magistrate mouthed some of Ham's words as though trying to make sense of the garbled speech. He finally remarked, "You are saying she and the others didn't do anything wrong? You want me to drop their warrants?"

Ham bobbed his head. "*Yessir*, I am the bum. Nickl Nackl is as fine as cream gravy, and the rest are no different. None of them would belong in a hoosegow, let alone have their necks stretched, *mmhmm*."

"Look at that," Adam snickered, "an honorable minotaur. I would not expect him to take the blame, but it doesn't matter. He cannot carry the load for every crime broken. They are guilty by accountability, at the very least." The captain folded his arms and stared at his brother. "If innocent, why run? Why would they fight alongside a criminal?"

With a guttural growl, Ham leaned closer to the captain

and spoke in his ear. "If you don't hobble your lip, I am going to clean your plow."

"A-are you threatening me?" The captain looked over his shoulder with a raised eyebrow, more confusion in his voice than contention.

"Reckon I am, *mmhmm.*"

Nickl slipped by the captain to the desk's edge, motioning for Charlie to lean forward and listen. He did not budge in his chair, but she spoke all the same with the authority of the noble family in which she was raised. "The adventuring life has its highs and lows, Magistrate. I am not saying that Ham and our company have not had our fair share of challenging situations, but we have done nothing in the spirit of being mean. We are tracking a deadly death-dealer, and—"

"A death-dealer?" The magistrate sprang forward, the feather in his hat swaying. His bulging eyes narrowed at the captain as though he were responsible for all the hate in the world. "Did you know they were after a death-dealer?"

Adam turned from Ham with a shrug. "They mentioned it, but it is rubbish. Nothing but a rumor they quickly incited, likely hoping we'd give them leniency."

"It is not a rumor." The magistrate scrambled to grab the papers beneath his hands, lifting them as though the evidence of Nickl's words were inscribed on the parchment. He waved them in the air. "Reports of undead and decaying crops and devilish fiends from the otherworld have been flooding my desk for weeks. It may be above your pay grade, but these are serious times and serious threats. These two champions are doing us a service by tracking down this monstrosity. And you would interrupt their quest!"

The captain spewed laughter. "Interrupt their quest? She was wandering the streets and he was drowning himself in whiskey. The only thing I interrupted were the acts of dawdling and debauchery. It is my duty to track the living, Magistrate, not fairy tales. Should I remind you again that it is your duty to sentence the living when I bring them to your doorstep? Perhaps I should contact Father after all. You don't have the stomach for your work."

"You bloodthirsty bastard." Charlie stiffened his upper lip, nostrils flaring, squinting at his brother. Adam only smiled slyly in return. With an exasperated breath, the magistrate leaned back in defeat, addressing Ham and Nickl. "I'm sorry. I would pardon you and let you go after this death-dealer, but it seems another fate awaits you."

He waved them off.

"No!" Nickl shouted. "Please, no!"

"You-you're making a mistake!" Ham slurred as the guards dragged him out the door.

He heard the captain laughing behind them. "See you next time, Cheddar."

In a flash, the entrance hall disappeared, and Ham was pushed out the wooden door into the throng of guards outside. They pushed and pulled him toward the gallows where the hanging noose awaited him; he could hear Nickl shouting frantically behind him, but all he could see was the many faces of the guards and their shiny helms.

It was not until Ham stomped up the stairs to the stage and was half-dragged to the center crate to stand upon that he noticed the crowd gathering in the streets. One of the guards began shouting out his and Nickl's crimes, flouting their champion status and disparaging them as low-life crooks. Ham blocked out the words, eyeing the ashen sky, its sun fading on the horizon. It offered an eerie ambiance; the buzz of the crowd only jostled his nerves more.

"Step up, minotaur," ordered the guard at his rear. His instinct was to fight—to turn around and smash the guard's face before freeing Nickl—but he did as he was instructed, hearing the creak of the crate under his weight. A moment later, Nickl stood perched on two stacked crates next to him, the hollow rope hanging inches above her head. The guards took their time pulling the nooses over their necks while the other continued to talk to the crowd about their inherent evilness.

Ham squinted to see Nickl on her toes, fighting to keep her balance on the crate with the rope around her neck, while he was not entirely sure his feet wouldn't hit the platform when his makeshift stool was removed. "I am sorry, Nickl," he choked. "It should have never so sour, but I guess we will get another chance soon enough."

Nickl's voice tremored, bobbing her head slightly. "We will be alright. It won't hurt for long."

Swallowing a lump in his throat, Ham watched the captain make his way up the stairs. A thin smile was frozen on his face, likely a remnant since he walked out of his brother's establishment moments ago. He approached Ham from behind, the smell of decay suddenly overwhelming Ham. He wondered why he had sensed nothing earlier; maybe it was the smell of whiskey burning in his nostrils.

The captain smacked his lips before saying, "No reason to draw this out."

Nickl's pitched gasp caused Ham to look over his shoulder.

Adam was too close, his face hidden behind Ham's shoulder, but Ham could see one thing—the skin cracking under Adam's left eye. The captain signaled to a guard to pull a lever at the back of the platform while rotten black ooze surfaced from under the broken flesh.

The captain was undead.

Ham's roar caught in his throat as a trapdoor opened under him and Nickl, and the noose tightened around his neck. Splotches of color filled his vision, blotching out the world around him as the crates crashed somewhere beneath. Losing control of his senses, he violently rocked his body, reaching for the rope with his hands to no avail; he could not get his thick fingers under the binding.

The crack of two gunshots sounded one after another. The pressure of the rope released, and Ham suddenly fell, smashing into the crate beneath him. The world spun as he tried to regain his senses, hearing more gunshots booming along with the screams of the bystanders. Footsteps could be heard in every direction, leaving him disoriented and confused.

"Ham..." Nickl said weakly.

Slackening the rope around his neck, Ham twisted to see the gnome girl. She lay bent over the broken pieces of her crate. Her eyes fluttered slightly while she tugged the rope over her head. Dust and debris danced through the air in the dim light spilling through the holes above. Ham saw the edge of the captain move from sight on the platform. The undead bastard shouted something unintelligible at the guard. More footsteps echoed.

"What in tarnation happened?"

"I-I don't know."

A familiar voice spouted behind him, "I shoots you down, muley!"

"Beans?" Ham cranked his head.

"Beans!" Nickl echoed.

The golden-haired gnome girl dipped her head, spinning a black-eyed Susan in her hand. "I told you I would be back. Now, Kildrak cannot hold them back for long. We have to go!"

"We aren't going nowhere till we put that captain six feet under," Ham snarled.

Beans lifted an eyebrow. "Methinks that killing is what got us into this to begin with, but if you wants to shoots him, I won't stop you."

"He is undead," Nickl said.

Beans smiled. "In that case, I will be shootsing him too."

11

Setting Things Right

DAY 180, 4023 CE

"Time to bust some skulls." Gunshots echoed above and around Ham. He cocked his head to look through the open trapdoor of the gallows and saw nothing more than the severed ropes he'd been hanging from moments earlier. Another gun boomed from the opposite side of the hatch, the lingering smoke from a fired barrel wafting into view. With a strained swallow, he squinted for some sign of Captain Adam. The undead bastard might have scurried off the stage, leaving his armored goons to fire at Kildrak—wherever the dwarf was hiding.

Suddenly, the citizens who had congregated on the streets to watch them hang screamed in panic, one after another, throughout what might have been the whole of Fosterhold. Ham tensed at the cacophony of sound, fearful that his and the gnome's presence beneath the gallows was the source of their sudden fear. Beans forcibly pushed by him with a huff.

"What are they yelling about?" she asked, peering through

the columned wood beneath the gallows. "Have they never seen a rescue before?"

Before Ham could reply, Nickl cried, "Get down!" Bullets flew on either side of them, rebounding off the beams. Beans turned as quickly as she had come, scrambling to Nickl's side behind Ham. He dipped down to protect them with his large frame, looking over his shoulder at the street beyond the wooden posts. At first, he thought the citizens were firing at them, but then he saw a line of guards marching closer, already pulling their rifles back to reload, while the people of the city wildly ran for shelter like ants fleeing from fire.

When the shooting subsided, Beans rose with Ham and Nickl, holding a six-shooter in either of her hands. "Would you take a look at that?" She pointed. "I don't recall you saying that all the guards were dead."

Ham narrowed his eyes, seeing the decayed skin and rot decorating their exposed skin—faces and hands—bespeaking their true nature. Whatever magic had hidden their features was fading away. A chuckle reverberated in his throat as he reached for his gun. "I reckon that gives us reason to kick up the dust, *mmhmm.*" He dipped his head to Beans, a wide smile cracking his lips. "You stay safe now, you hear?"

"I will be fine," she replied. "I did not come all the way back to be killed again."

He tore the blunderbuss free from its leather holster and fired. Beans followed suit and fired two rounds right after him. The enemy echoed their sentiment, sending a barrage of bullets back at them. Every shot from either side missed.

Nickl pulled her daggers free. "Why do you two even carry those boomsticks? You never hit anything." Dashing from under the gallows, she rushed the nearest guard while Ham hurried to reload his blunderbuss. Her daggers plunged into the guard's stomach, its black insides spewing outward as she ripped them across his gut.

The undead let loose an unearthly screech and clawed at Nickl. Ham's heart stopped in his chest as the sharp nails cut through the air inches from her face. He exhaled loudly when its head exploded, a bullet ripping through the back of its skull and out from between its eyes. Following the trajectory, Ham located Kildrak lying flat on a roof on the opposite side of the road, the rifle perched upon his shoulder.

Beans squealed with excitement and waved at Kildrak before lifting her guns and firing again. One bullet hit the guard nearest to Nickl, while the other vanished into the swarming crowd.

Ham squeezed his way between the columns and shot his blunderbuss at the same undead guard. The slug tore through his neck, but the scum stayed on his feet. Sluggishly, the guard stumbled forward and swiped at Nickl with as much ferocity as the first guard, this time striking her across the face. She yelled in pain, whipping her head sideways where bloodied marks carved across her cheek.

The line of undead fired their guns once more. Most of the spread missed them, but a single bullet buried itself in Ham's thigh. Nickl's second antagonized whelp kept his mind off his own pain. The dark-haired gnome gripped her gut with a single hand. Blood pooled around her fingers where a bullet had lodged itself. The color drained from her face.

"No!" Ham bellowed. He would not let her or anyone else

in their party die again. He rocked his head side to side, waiting for his turn so he could storm forward to protect her.

Another well-aimed shot from Kildrak ripped through the monster's skull, dropping it to the earth with a thud.

"She will be alright," Beans assured him. Ham watched Nickl stumble back, reach for a liquid blue at her belt, and down it. Some of her color returned as Beans cocked her guns.

Ham grunted in response, scanning the array of guards on the street and then an additional two—also undead—lurking on the platform behind him. "Where did that yellow-bellied captain scamper off to?"

"Don't you worry about it, muley. We'll find him, but right now, you need to take your turn so I can shoots something."

Ham eyed the battlefield and realized everything was frozen, waiting on him to fire his gun or move closer. He raked his eyes at the space between Nickl and the handful of encroaching guards with their weapons poised to fire. No doubt she would be the target of their attack if he did not do something.

Dropping his blunderbuss to the dirt, Ham charged at the nearest guard. He swung with a closed fist, missing his mark completely, and then bounded to the next enemy. The guard behind him awkwardly swatted at him with the butt of his gun, missing him as he stomped away. He headbutted the second guard squarely in the forehead, dropping him to the ground with a single blow. He approached the third guard with a guttural roar, stepping directly in front of the loaded weapon with a snarl.

"Ham!" Nickl wailed.

Her warning was too late as the guards fixated their fire

on him. Time and again, the firearms exploded around him like cannons, sending waves of smoke billowing into the air and leaving a distinct ringing in his ears. When the commotion died down, Ham slid his hands over his front and arms, finding that there were no additional holes. The undead guard directly in front of him gaped with dead eyes, dropping its gaze to the double-barrel against Ham's chest. How he missed the point-blank shot was beyond understanding.

Ham broadened his grin. "Our turn."

Two of Nickl's daggers spun in Ham's peripheral, stabbing into the skull of a guard to his left. Ham did not bother watching him fall, instead smashing his head into the confused foe in front of him. The undead staggered a step and Ham hit him again for good measure. As he took his last breath, a third farther back crumbled after being shot by Beans and Kildrak.

With a small jeer, Ham nodded with approval. If they kept hitting like this, they would win this fight without any trouble. Only a few more guards remained in the streets.

Several shots flew overhead when Ham heard Beans yowl. He twisted to see her reaching for her shoulder—one of the guards standing on the gallows had shot her. She dipped down, likely close to dropping from the single shot. She was not as high level as the rest of them; she was lucky to be standing toe-to-toe with any of them.

Snarling, he turned around, finally seeing Captain Adam standing between the two riflemen, a sneer of his own painted upon his rotting face.

He flashed his blackened teeth, dark bile seeping through his lips as he spoke. "The law will be upheld. If you won't die by hanging, perhaps you'd prefer to die by fire!" Flames threateningly lashed from the tips of the captain's fingers but did not have the range to touch any of them.

"Blast him in his frying pan, Kildrak!"

Not wasting any time, Ham thundered forward and slammed his might into the beams holding the gallows. Already weakened by the continued misfire, the first column snapped in two with ease and the second groaned against his unrelenting force. The stage above him shook and swayed; the thumping of the undead stomping around in an attempt to keep their balance was music to his ears.

After hearing the dwarf fire his weapon from the rooftops, a single rifleman crashed through the trapdoor of the gallows and landed at Ham's feet. Even with a hole through its chest, the undead was not defeated, but Ham was too focused on breaking the column to bother with the bastard.

As it began to stir on the ground, Nickl came sliding in next to Ham and planted her dagger in its chest, stealing the remainder of its life. She looked to Beans and pointed above her with untamed eagerness. "Knock down the other one!"

"No, Beans!" Ham rumbled, looking at the golden-haired dwarf struggling to stand. "Take a liquid blue."

Ham grimaced as Beans spun the black-eyed Susans in her hands. "Oh! I'll shoots 'em!"

"Bea—" Ham could not protest quick enough before her weapons went off in succession, sending slugs flying at the enemy above him. He heard a deathly grunt from above, yet neither the captain nor the remaining rifleman fell through the trapdoor.

The three guards who remained in the streets turned on

them. The first raised its weapon at Beans and fired, the bullet grazing a hair over her shoulder and missing. Ham sighed with relief, hoping she would take a liquid blue on her next turn. One shot would have sent her back to level one again. The second and third guards fired their weapons at him. The bullets struck the beams on either side of him, sending wood shrapnel flying into the air.

Ham raised an eyebrow. "Dang! What a bunch of small potatoes. Couldn't hit the broad side of a barn if they were standing inside it, *mmhmm*." Kildrak and Beans returned fire, producing death cries from the enemy behind him, while Ham returned his focus to snapping the support against his shoulder. With a final heave, he pushed through the thick wood.

"It's all going to fall," Nickl screeched, skedaddling back away from Ham and out from under the gallows.

Ham saw the entire frame veer sideways, the structure snapping and popping. Dust and debris fell over him. With a concerned yell, he pushed off his hooves with what strength he could muster and followed Nickl, who ran directly toward the remaining guard in the street. Behind him, he heard a crash as though something fell through the hole, but he did not have time to look. His guess was the last undead rifleman did not make it out alive.

He made it two steps beyond the piling rubble before the captain landed in the dirt within arm's length, sending up dust in all directions.

Nickl squawked an incomprehensible battle cry, leaping into the final guard and plunging her daggers into its belly.

Ham twisted to face the captain, who stood with a squinting eye and smelled like the backside of a horse.

He jerked a sword from his belt and pointed it at Ham. "You will not make it out of this alive."

Ham looked around at his friends. "Odds are I will, *mmhmm.*"

The captain slashed his sword at Ham. Once. Twice. Three times. Two of the strikes ripped into Ham's chest.

HAMROGENI "HAM" HERDSTOMPER			LEVEL 3	4605/6000
MEDIUM	MINOTAUR	BARBARIAN	CHAOTIC EVIL	60
POWER	16		HP	12/33
DEXERTITY	14		ARMOR	13
ENDURANCE	14			
INTELLIGENCE	6		SKILLS	SPELLS
AWARENESS	8		INTIMIDATE	IDENTIFY
CHARISMA	4		SURVIVAL	MARKSMAN
LUCK	2		SEAFARING	
			INTERCEPT	
DEFECT	BLOOD LEAF ADDICTION		CHIPS	220

The pain was excruciating. With blood running down his chest, he pulled up his stat sheet to check his health. He knew he could not continue like this much longer, yet he could not stop himself from smiling. His alignment had ticked up slightly back to *good*. He tried to sound menacing. "You are making me madder than an old wet hen, you son of a gun. I hope you are ready for a real lickin'."

Kildrak fired two shots from the rooftop and surprisingly missed them both, followed by Beans, who wildly shot to the left of the captain.

"Shitfire!" Ham shouted.

Nickl than somersaulted behind the captain and swung her two daggers at his back, also missing both attacks.

With a roar, Ham swung both meaty fists and missed too! He damn near believed the undead bastard was invisible. The captain took his turn again, focused solely on Ham with three swings of his sword. This time, however, the sword ignited into flames before slicing across Ham's midsection. He was lucky only one of the three attacks hit him. The fire damage tore through him, cutting what life he had left in half.

He searched for some insult to throw at the smirking captain, the world fading with his diminishing life. "You—you're dead meat."

Kildrak fired once more with his pepperbox rifle, missing entirely. Ham swore he could hear the dwarf grumbling to himself as he threw the weapon off the rooftop and picked up the smoking blunderbuss they acquired at Braewood Keep. Taking aim, he fired again. This time, he struck true. Captain Adam's head snapped back, skin tearing off his face from the impact.

Beans fired from behind and missed again and again, but Nickl was able to plunge a blade near the captain's spine. Adam cringed, black gunk spilling from his mouth in excess.

Ham smiled, stepping into Adam's space. With a snarl, he slammed his head forward and smashed Adam's skull. Without remorse, he grabbed the jacket and smashed the captain again with enough force to burrow a hole down to his nose bone.

The captain died.

"Wow, Ham," Nickl whispered as he dropped the limp body. "I think we got him."

He wiped the muck from his brow. "I reckon it's time we go finish off the death-dealer now."

"If—if you do," a quivering voice floated from a doorway beyond the gallows, "I would be willing to exonerate any charges against you and your friends."

"Cheddar..." Ham identified the magistrate.

He cleared his throat, correcting him. "Charlie." The magistrate slowly examined the bloodied scene, his dead brother lying under Ham. His voice carried off, saying, "He got what he deserved."

"You are gonna exon...exoner..." Ham furrowed his brow at the word.

"He is going to pardon us, Ham," Nickl explained.

Ham grinned, looking up at the yellow rays beaming through the white clouds. "Well, in that case, we best go make hay while the sun still shines, *mmhmm*."

12

On the Road Again

The woods were pleasantly quiet, save the sound of the travelers' footsteps. Ham glanced over his companions one at a time, feeling his heart swell with delight. Kildrak led them with his pepperbox rifle slung over his shoulder. Nickl followed behind with a bit of a hop in her step, grinning at the sunrays dancing across her face. And Beans strutted alongside Ham, holding the smoking blunderbuss in her left hand. Her surefire grip hadn't loosened since retrieving it from Kildrak.

Ham's eyes lingered on her the longest.

"You've been giving me that look since I returned two days ago, muley." She smiled. "I told you I would come back."

"Sure you did," Ham agreed with a subtle nod, "but I did not believe you. That is to say, I did not believe it was possible. How would you know to look for us after being incarnated again?" Ham offered a blank stare, unable to remember the slew of companions he and Nickl had seen come and go over the many lives they had lived as champions. "Have we ever had a party member come back to us again, Nickl?"

Nickl did not miss a beat in her reply. "No, not intentionally anyway. We have crossed some old friends on the road and traveled alongside one another for a time. Remember Goldie and Shroedinger? We had some great adventures!" Nickl shrugged her small shoulders. "But usually it is not worth tracking past party members down. The difference in our levels makes it impossible. The challenge rating of new monsters is simply too great to have the lower-level champion in the party."

He was lucky enough to remember Nickl each go-around, and it was usually because she found him. He had no idea who these other champions were that she mentioned. Ham cleared his throat and weakly said, "Beans seems to be holding her own."

Nickl nodded in agreement.

"Of course I hold my own!" Beans scrunched up her brow. "Each time I reincarnate I make a point of asking Mister Sammich what I was doing last; that is, after the character creation fog clears up. I am a champion! I don't think it is right for me to leave my friends behind. It is an important piece of my back story."

Ham scratched at his forehead. "*Hmm.* How did you come by us to begin with if you always return to your previous party? You know, when we met you at Clery."

"I had only recently come back." Beans blinked several times as though she were batting tears away, but maybe she was simply trying to remember. Nevertheless, her voice choked as she went on, saying, "I died during the battle with the final boss, but my previous party survived and advanced to NPC status. I did not have anyone to return to."

"That is s-so sad," Nickl stammered.

"It's okay." Beans beamed. "I have you now."

"We are glad you are back," Kildrak piped up from the front. "No way we could fight the death-dealer without you with us."

"I reckon not, *mmhmm*," Ham said, "but we would do better to get Beans leveled up another time or two before we go storming into Braewood Keep. Should we stand out here and knock some wolves in the head or something?"

"That would take weeks." Nickl shuddered, sticking her tongue out.

Ham lifted his finger. "Better to take weeks strengthening our position than rushing in and dying. No one wants to spend months getting back to this point again. I am tired of all this champion business."

"Me too," Nickl said.

"We should have another few battles before the death-dealer," Kildrak said, adjusting the rifle on his shoulder again. "It will be higher level monsters with more experience, which should level Beans well enough. I don't think we need to go chasing after first-level beasts."

"I don't know," Nickl said. "It has been quiet for a couple of days."

A bloodcurdling scream pitched from beyond the trees ahead, followed by the clanging sounds of swords and gunfire.

"You had to say something." Ham grimaced. "C'mon, let's go get some experience."

Caring little for stealth, he barreled pass Kildrak toward

the ruckus. A death cry resounded as he squeezed between two trees to see a small array of travelers. Two men lay dead with their rifles in the dirt by their hands, a human girl barely bigger than Nickl held another rifle, and an older woman huddled behind a younger lady to protect two children. The younger lady raised her gun to fire at the horde of undead assailing upon them.

"Keep firing, Lucy!" The young lady instructed, pulling the trigger of her own weapon. The boomstick sent a slug through the nearest zombie's head.

Lucy—not old enough to be an adult—did as she was told and dropped a second that staggered closer through the trees. "I am, Jillian. I am!"

Beans and Kildrak's guns resounded on either side of Ham, hitting their marks with ease, but Ham was not sure it would be enough. He counted a dozen and a half of the undead. They were severely outnumbered.

"Nickl." He looked over his shoulder. "I reckon you better ready one of those bombs of yours or this is going to be as difficult as skinning a possum alive."

"No problem." She fished in her pocket and pulled out a makeshift explosive.

With a satisfied nod, Ham lifted his blunderbuss and fired it into the fray. He was not surprised when he missed the shot. "Tarnation! I can't remember the last time I hit anything with this blasted gun."

"Just use your head, Ham," Nickl said.

Ham tossed the gun to the ground, taking several strides to the closest undead to use his second attack. The sickening crack reverberated in Ham's ears as he connected with the skull of his enemy. When he pulled back, he could see the dent in the undead bastard's skull, but it remained standing. He clearly did not hit it hard enough.

The walking dead ambled from what seemed like every direction, emerging from the trees like a nefarious fog. They turned their attention from the travelers to Ham and his friends. The throaty gurgles coming from the swarm of undead sounded wet and irregular like a mass of sops spilling their insides simultaneously after a disastrous night of untamed debauchery.

Kildrak grunted as he was hit from behind, followed by a frightened squeal from Beans. Ham jerked to her with worry, his insides twisting, but noticed she had dodged the clawed hand raking at her face. Nickl echoed with a similar sound, shoving her bomb back into her pocket and swinging her daggers at the undead closing in on either side. Her blades struck the rotten meat only to have the droopy-faced monsters hit her right back.

Several undead attacked Ham, surprisingly missing even though he was distracted by his companions' well-being. He snorted, looking to the children and women to his left; the women looked at him almost fearfully while reloading their guns.

"Do not be frightened now, *mmhmm*," Ham said hastily, pausing at the sight of the dead kin at their feet. The young children with the older woman were sobbing. He searched for something encouraging to say. "We will make short work of these wicked yellowbellies."

Jillian and Lucy fired their guns again. While Jillian

missed her shot, Lucy dropped the zombie in front of Ham. She was a damn fine shooter for being so young.

He swallowed hard, glad the bullet hit its mark and not him instead. He nodded at the young girl who broadly grinned at him. "Good...good shot."

Fighting the urge to turn around and watch his friends fight, Ham focused on the staggering zombies that approached him and the numerous others that spilled from the trees. Round after round, he swung and smashed his head at the gathering mound of undead. Time and again, he missed as though their physical form were nonexistent, completely ethereal. As luck would have it, none of them seemed capable of hitting him either.

Kildrak and Beans fired their guns in succession, and then Nickl shouted victoriously as she dropped another enemy. Ham frowned, twisting his head. Two lifeless bodies slumped at her feet and he had barely done a lick of damage.

Ham swung a fist at the undead in front of him twice more and missed again. "Dodgasted, black-blooded mudhills!"

The first three undead around him clawed and gnashed their teeth at the air, but the fourth one finally made contact, smacking Ham across the mouth hard enough to draw blood. Ham growled as two well-aimed shots from Lucy and Jillian tore the zombie in half. It died instantly.

The sounds of the grating undead and firing guns danced around him while he waited for his turn. He heard Nickl groan as one of the monsters struck her, but she did not seem to be concerned by the superficial cut left on her neck. When Ham had the chance to act again, he presented his best snarl at the hollow-eyed scum that stood toe-to-toe with him.

"I have had about enough of this," he said. Using his maximum strength, he headbutted the first with enough force to snap its neck and then slugged the second hard enough to send it flying into a nearby tree. Both died immediately, leaving the single undead in front of him. Ham pointed at him. "You're next."

Jillian and Lucy fired at the monster as though they might steal his chance to tan its hide, but their slugs flew well overhead of the bone-bag. More undead fell behind him as Beans, Nickl, and Kildrak repeatedly hit their target.

When the zombie missed its attack against Ham, he took his first attack with too much fervor, swiping at the air. But his second attack struck true, knocking the jaw clean off the head and dropping the body. The remainder of the undead fell one after another behind him.

"I reckon that's it—" Ham's smile was cut short by an ear-piercing screech emanating from the two dead caravan members, one after the other, as they rigidly sat upright. Their white eyes and thin black lips dripped dark goop—they were no longer among the living.

"Pa!" Lucy wailed as the younger children screamed and hid their eyes in the older woman's clothing.

"Billie!" The younger woman belted out right after.

"Get back!" Ham ordered, seeing Kildrak and Beans swinging the end of their guns toward the newly undead. The screech was parroted by a handful more zombies suddenly appearing in the trees almost thirty feet away.

"They just keep coming!" Kildrak wiped blood from a gash beneath his right eye with the back of his hand.

"Nickl," Ham started.

She was already ahead of him, revealing the black powder bomb from her pocket and lighting it.

The next moment happened so fast that Ham barely caught sight of everyone's actions. Nickl lobbed the bomb over Ham's head toward the emerging mass of undead, while Kildrak, Jillian, Beans, and Lucy fired their weapons at the revived dead at the feet of the travelers. The horde was blown to smithereens in a sudden flash of light and smoke, while two bullets ripped through each of the undead men, killing them...again.

Lucy threw down her gun as the men fell, emotion overwhelming her and tears like those of the children suddenly seeping from her eyes. "Oh..." she started, falling to her haunches and burying her face in her hands.

"They're dead." Jillian rushed to the old woman and children near the bloodied corpses of their kin. She grabbed the children and hugged them tight as though the green fabric of her cloak could forever protect them from the ghastly images that surrounded them.

Ham looked at each. In this part of the sentence, an addition like "of his company, more grateful than even that they had survived. He traipsed closer to Lucy and followed the example set by Jillian, wrapping his arms around the small girl. His voice shook. "I am so sorry for your loss, young'un. Truly I am."

The blue in her eyes was blurred from her pooling tears. "Tell me that you are the good guys. Tell me that you're going to stop the death-dealer."

Ham gripped her tighter. "To tell you the truth, for a spell, I wasn't too sure who was good and who wasn't, but I reckon it don't matter too much. I know now that we here have the sand to do what needs to be done, *mmhmm*. So y'all get on back to town and be safe." Ham squinted one eye with intensity, looking to the road leading to Braewood. "As for us, come heaven or hellfire, we're gonna go bed down that death-dealer."

13

Death's Doorstep

The rest of the journey to Braewood Keep took longer than it should have with battles against the undead awaiting them around every bend. Between crushing skulls and finding a safe place to rest, Ham had found little time to do much else, even to take a gander at his stat sheet. With the black towers of Braewood Keep now peeking over the trees, he had the urge to check his alignment but quickly decided against it.

The wave of joy in his chest told him all he needed to know. He was with his friends on a road to redemption, to restitution, to righteousness. No matter what his alignment showed, he was exactly where he belonged.

"I have not seen you touch the blood leaf since I returned, muley." Beans tilted her head up to him. "Did you give it up?"

At the mention of the drug, Ham sniffed instinctively, his fingers twitching at his side. He had done his best to forget about the blood leaf and the booze. The alcohol consumption had helped him cope with some of the shakes and sweats, but with nothing running through his system and the constant fighting in recent days, his body felt heavy. "I have a packet left. I considered using it against the death-dealer."

He fought back the thoughts to pull the final packet from his pouch and snort it.

"What about after?" Beans asked.

Ham shook his head. "No. One more time and that is it."

Nickl touched his arm. "I am proud of you, Ham."

"Whoa." Kildrak stopped ahead of them, lifting his hand as though he were halting a team of horses. The din of gurgling and groaning undead drifted through the trees ahead, leading to the front doors of Braewood Keep. "How are we looking?"

He revealed his stat sheet to check the numbers.

KILDRAK TORUNN			LEVEL 4	6500/9000
MEDIUM	DWARF	MARKSMAN	CHAOTIC GOOD	'170

POWER	10		HP	34/34
DEXERTITY	10		ARMOR	12
ENDURANCE	16			
INTELLIGENCE	8		SKILLS	SPELLS
AWARENESS	12		PERCEPTION	-
CHARISMA	6		SHARPSHOOTER	-
LUCK	4		HISTORY	
			AIMED SHOT	
DEFECT	FEMALE NPCS		CHIPS	1210

Nickl and Beans followed his example, showing their increased levels, hit points, and new abilities. The journey had enhanced their wherewithal more than Ham had thought.

NICKL NACKLE			LEVEL 4	6200/9000
SMALL	GNOME	ROUGE	CHAOTIC NEURAK	'75

POWER	6		HP	27/27
DEXERTITY	16		ARMOR	10
ENDURANCE	8			
INTELLIGENCE	12		SKILLS	SPELLS
AWARENESS	14		INVESTIGATE	-
CHARISMA	12		SNEAK	-
LUCK	4		EXPLOSIVES	
			SHADOW MELD	
DEFECT	*EASILY FRIGHTENED*		CHIPS	705

BEANS			LEVEL 3	3200/6000
MEDIUM	GNOME	GUN ENTHUSIAST	CHAOTIC EVIL	'40

POWER	6		HP	26/26
DEXERTITY	14		ARMOR	9
ENDURANCE	8			
INTELLIGENCE	16		SKILLS	SPELLS
AWARENESS	10		PERCEPTION	-
CHARISMA	12		SHARPSHOOTER	-
LUCK	6		HISTORY	
DEFECT	*STEALING*		CHIPS	120

Kildrak nodded with approval and then looked at Ham expectantly.

"Don't worry about me none. I am right as rain, *mmhmm.*" Ham cleared his throat. "Now let's go in there and make sure we don't make a mux of it this time."

Rustling his mustache with a twitch of his lip, Kildrak turned back to the trees. "Well, alright then. It sounds like there are a handful lingering outside. Do we want to fight them or make a run for the door?"

"We might do better to save our energy for the final battle," Nickl said. "We are exhausted enough as it is."

Ham snorted. "We didn't come here to leave any of these dang dead walking. I say we slaughter every last one of them."

"We either kill them now or on the way," Beans said. "Might as well shoots them down while we have the strength."

"Well, I guess that settles it." Kildrak placed the butt of his pepperbox rifle against his shoulder and checked that it was loaded. "Let's...uh...*shoots* them."

Beans beamed.

Nickl laughed under breath, pulling her daggers from her belt. She scooted ahead of Kildrak and ducked into the green foliage. "Time to get stabby." Ham blinked a couple times as she disappeared in front of his eyes. He had not looked too closely at her stat sheet, but she must have acquired a new skill in the past couple days.

Ham kicked up dirt with his hooves and led them through the brush, the gigantic closed doors leading into Braewood Keep quickly coming into view. The black square towers on either side of the fortress loomed overhead, as intimidating now as they had been when they first approached this edifice of death.

But his focus was on the mindless dead that swirled haphazardly around to meet their charge. Ham reached the first before it fully turned, and he headbutted it hard enough to knock the life force from its hide with ease. "Like lickin' butter off a knife."

Kildrak was quick on the trigger, striking a zombie to Ham's left with a well-executed headshot. "We got the jump on them. Make it count!"

Two quick shots boomed behind Ham as Beans slung lead at another undead fiend. The first missed, but the second rattled its bone cage. It did not drop immediately, but a half-breath later Nickl appeared behind the bag of bones. She plunged a knife in its side, draining the remainder of its hit points.

"Three down." Nickl moved back behind Ham, eyeing the ground between them and the gate. "Only four more, and they are weaker than the ones we were fighting."

"Must be leftovers from the low-level hordes," Kildrak agreed, raising his pepperbox rifle again.

The first skeleton rushed toward Nickl with a ghastly whine. Ham was quick to use his Intercept ability, knocking the head clean off the lumbering bastard.

The last three attacked Ham with surprising ferocity, each one striking him, the last one hitting him hard enough to see stars. He gasped in shock, feeling his hit points slip away. "Low-level, my hairy ass."

He snarled and slammed his head into the first zombie, startling it, and then swung at its jaw with his fist to finish it. The skeleton somehow swayed, and Ham missed the swing, looking like a half-brained mop. Lead plumbs soared on either side of him from Kildrak and Beans, every bullet missing its target.

"What in tarnation!" he screamed.

"We don't want to shoots you, muley!" Beans retorted.

"I don't want you shootin' me neither. I want you to shoot these goddamn lanky bastards right here in front of me, *mmhmm.*"

Nickl's battle cry drowned Ham's words as she swung her daggers wildly at the foes in front of him, the blades not even coming close to the beasts.

Ham swallowed a mouthful of spit. All three were going to get to attack him again. He dropped his eyes to Nickl, feeling fear grip his heart. "And what is your excuse?"

She grimaced, looking down. "Sorry."

The skeletons took their turn clawing at Ham without remorse. Three times their bony nails ripped across his chest. Thick red blood oozed down his fur.

"Oh, hellfire. It burns." His head spun; his knees grew weak.

With what strength he could muster, he swiped twice at the injured skeleton. His second blow landed, killing it.

No sooner had it touched the dirt than a bullet burst through the skeleton's head to his left. Bone shrapnel flew in every direction, ricocheting off Ham's large frame.

One more.

Ham faced the ghastly beast about the time Beans' shots soared over its head.

"Don't worry, Ham," Nickl squealed. "No way I can miss again." Tumbling behind the skeleton, she swiped her daggers twice and struck true. With her second motion, her blade cut through the twisted spine to end the fight.

Ham breathed slow, holding his wounds. "Anyone have any liquid blue?"

Beans reached in her bag. "I have a dozen or so. Take a seat and you can start gulping these down."

By and by, the doors shut and the four of them faced the familiar hall ahead that would lead them to the death-dealer atop the tower. Debris and the dead littered the corridor from their previous excursion.

"Well," Kildrak rumbled from behind Ham, his speech

slow as he reflected on the happenings that led them into the keep, "that was all unexpected." He cleared his throat. "I hope the rest of this goes smoothly."

Ham blinked a few times, rolling his shoulders in preparation. Despite everything, his hit points were at max and his companions looked to be in good shape. "We might be so worn out that we have a hankering for the longest rest you've ever seen, but sure as a gun—no matter what happens—we are going to survive this. Every last one of us."

"And we will be NPCs at the end of it." Nickl grinned. "No more champion life."

"No more," Ham agreed and started forward.

The four of them trudged on without a word. When they came to the area where Beans had died from the cursed blue gem, Ham hustled forward as though lingering too long might bring about a repeat fate. Images of her pained face and the stone melting into a gauntlet of death seared into his mind, tempting him to reach for the last packet of blood leaf. He wanted to be rid of those memories forever.

Yet a simple touch from Nickl pulled him back to reality, her hand clasping his own, and his heart boldened. He would not let anything happen to Beans again. He would not anything happen to any of them. Not today.

Through two levels of the keep, Ham heard nothing but the sound of their own breathing and footsteps. Where the halls had been filled with undead before, Braewood Keep was now silent as a grave. He began to wonder if they would find the death-dealer at the top of the tower when a sharp pain touched his heart.

He paused, a surprised wheeze escaping his lips as he clutched his chest.

A similar noise came from Kildrak, Beans, and Nickl.

"What is happening?" Kildrak coughed, looking to the walls with wide eyes. It was as though he expected the stone to begin bleeding.

"We must be getting close," Nickl said, forcing herself to take a step ahead of Ham.

"H-he is not going to be easy to kill," Beans said, checking the smoking blunderbuss with a wry eye. "But I'll die trying."

Ham scowled, reaching for the blood leaf packet. It was time. "No. One. Is. Dying."

14

The Showdown

The blood leaf flowed through Ham as though it were his first time inhaling the powdery red substance. He sucked in a mouthful of air, bracing himself as a sudden surge of energy rippled from his hooves to his head. His heart thudded in his chest and his mind swarmed with static; his muscles flexed against his will. With a loud exhale, he realized how ready, almost eager he was for the death dealer. In this moment, he did not give two licks if the undead bastard threw lightning at him. He would catch the bolt between his teeth and then throw it right back.

Ham fronted the line, directing them to the top of the tower with Nickl behind him, then Beans, and Kildrak holding the rear. The walls blurred by him as he pushed forward. With the blood leaf churning through him, he could not risk it running its course before the final battle was over.

"My chest is on fire." Kildrak groaned.

"It is going to get worse the closer we get," Beans replied.

Ham rocked his head from side to side, feeling the intensity of the death-dealer's presence in his body like his companions. He pulled his blunderbuss free, hoping he could shoot straight for once in this harrowing adventure. "Don't be gettin' afeared now. I reckon the death-dealer will have some aura of dread that we will have to bypass before tanning his hide. I don't want to be seeing any of you cutting stick when he shows his ugly mug, *mmhmm.*"

"We won't have much of a choice, Ham," Nickl said. "We either have the will to withstand it or we don't."

"All the same. Stand your ground."

Ham stepped over a shattered skeleton and twisted around the final curve leading to a thick wooden door that undoubtedly opened to the final room. Glowing black runes were inscribed on the door, seemingly pulsating against the wood. As Ham and the others neared, the markings throbbed harder, rattling the hinges.

Nickl grabbed Ham's hand, stopping him from advancing closer. The others stopped behind her. "I—I don't know about this. The door must be magically trapped, and we don't have a spellcaster in our party."

"She is right," Kildrak said. "I don't see any way of getting around this without blowing ourselves to smithereens."

"Smithereens? Horseshit! Unless you can read those runes, we can't have any idea what will happen. They may be just for show to scare us." Ham did not miss his companions subsequently raising their eyebrows in disbelief. "Watch me bust right through that door and I'll show y'all what's what, *mmhmm.*"

"Hold on, muley," Beans said. "Why don't I shoots it with

this before you go and knock yourself senseless?" She held up the smoking blunderbuss. "It got us through the front door well enough."

Kildrak tugged at his beard. "You did rattle your noggin for nothing the last time you tried to bust a door down."

"I busted through a pillar of wood well enough in Foster-hold and I am higher level now."

Nickl clicked her tongue, adding, "We need your hit points at max before going through the door or we are all dead. It isn't worth the risk."

"Dagnabbit. Does this have to happen with every final boss battle? I don't want to stand around all day arguing what strategy is best!" Ham twitched, a low hum suddenly sounding from the other side of the door. "Hear that? The death-dealer is now readying up for us because we are wasting time. We have lost the element of surprise."

"We cannot go barging in," Nickl said. "That is how we die and get reborn again. We need some sort of plan."

"I am not going to stop you from shooting it," Ham blurted with wide eyes. After half a breath, he waved his blunderbuss at Beans. "Shoot it already!"

The blonde-haired gnome smirked, spun the gun around in her small hand, and then fired at the *trapped* door behind Ham. The slug tore through the wood creating a hole the size of Ham's finger, and from that singular spot, crevices spiderwebbed across the surface of the wood. Ham covered his face with his arm as dense smoke suddenly spewed toward them from the cracks in a ghastly wave. The screeching of a thousand ghouls rattled Ham's eardrums. *BANG!* The door exploded, sending minuscule pieces of wooden shrapnel spraying in every direction harmlessly, like droplets of a spring rain. The smoke dispersed.

Ham cleared his throat and knocked the dust from his chest.

"Well, that did it," Kildrak said.

Grunting again, Ham advanced and entered the open doorway. Dim candlelight greeted him, emitting a subdued carroty hue over the rectangular room. The balls of wax were positioned strategically within a pentagram painted in blood in the center of the room. The light almost seemed to pulsate, illuminating the dark-clad figure at the heart of the design. The death-dealer's black tattered cloak rippled sinisterly from an unseen wind, causing the light of the room to flicker all the quicker. As Ham's eyes fell on it, a guttural laugh—deep and foreboding—escaped from beneath the shadowed hood.

Despite the darkness, he swore he could see the shape of the death-dealer's baleful smile.

"What do you see, muley?" Beans asked from the rear. "Is the death-dealer in there?"

"He must be." Nickl's voice trembled. "My heart is on fire with fear."

Ham snarled. "He's here."

Kildrak poked Ham in the back with his gun. "Well, get a move on. We cannot get a clear shot with you blocking the door."

"I can't," Ham said. "The round has started."

"Well, what are we waiting for?" Beans asked.

Nickl offered an explanation. "I think Ham needs to say something to the death-dealer to trigger the final fight. You know, where we figure out why he is raising the dead and attacking the living or why he is holed up here in Braewood Keep."

"Hell, I don't care about any of that," Ham muttered.

"Maybe he used to live here and was mistreated by locals and now he is back for revenge," Kildrak suggested.

"Or he could be an underworld servant of a greater demon overlord," Beans said.

"Oh no! That would send us to a bigger adventure after this one," Nickl gasped. "I want to be done after all this."

Kildrak continued to muse. "I bet he was a sorcerer who lived in this keep centuries ago and had his grave disrupted by some ornery kids. They probably took something that belongs to him and he wants it back."

"I don't care why he is here!" Ham reiterated.

"You have to say something so we can start the round," Nickl said. "You are at the front of the party. He cannot even see us."

Ham bit his inner cheek, momentarily searching for something worthwhile to say. Finally, his throaty words echoed across the chamber in a half holler. "Hey there, dead meat! If you think you're 'bout as ugly as a mud fence now, wait till me and my friends are done tanning your rotten backside, *mmhmm*. That's right! Even if you survive this ass whoopin', the sourest-looking bastards in the darkest graves won't lick your boots no more, you hear? You will be nothing to nobody! Nothing but a miserable, lonely flea—all by its lonesome—in the decaying folds of a decrepit bedroll, *mmhmm*."

A roar rang from under the death-dealer's hood with enough intensity to shake the stone walls.

"I don't understand half of what you just said..." Kildrak said.

"I said he's about as pretty as my ass after a week-long case of the runs," Ham stifled a chortle, "which is an upturn when compared to what we are about to do to him."

Kildrak grumbled under his breath. "Well, sounds like it did the trick."

The death-dealer immediately began chanting under its hood in a dead language unfamiliar to Ham, casting a spell of some sort. Ham couldn't know what magic would be cast or how long it would take to finish, but he found himself feeling lighter weight. Rocking his hornless head from side to side, he embraced the empowering effect of the blood leaf and charged at the death-dealer.

He only made it a few steps before the candles lighting the room started lashing fire at him. Two of the flames struck him, robbing him of a handful of hit points each, but two others missed him completely. Ignoring the pain, Ham leaped into the core of the pentagram and headbutted the death-dealer, expecting their skulls to crack.

But the death-dealer disappeared, and the frayed cloak fell to the ground. Ham spun around to see the undead sorcerer standing in the corner on the opposite side.

"He's over there!" Ham shouted.

Beans scooted through the door, hugging the wall to keep away from the candles, and fired at the death-dealer. Again, it vanished, only to appear in another corner of the room.

"Another specter." She scrunched her nose. "Shoot it, Kildrak."

The dwarf stomped into the room, taking the opposite

wall by the doorway, wasting no time in firing at their enemy. Ham's jaw fell as the target shimmered from existence once more.

"Where did it go now?" Kildrak widened his eyes.

"On me!" Beans screeched.

Ham looked over his shoulder to see the death-dealer hovering a hand's length away from the small gnomish girl.

"I got it," Nickl cried, somersaulting into the room and springing to Beans's side. With quick hands, she slashed her daggers side to side. The first swing missed the dark mass in front of her, but the second one struck into the robes, eliciting an unearthly screech from the undead. Nickl visibly gulped. "Why did this have to be the real one?"

"Tarnation." Ham grimaced. The two gnomes were across the room and it was the enemy's turn. Neither him nor Kildrak were close enough to do anything to protect them.

A clawed hand raked across Beans's face, tearing through her cheek and splashing blood across the floor. Ham's stomach dropped, watching the death-dealer tense momentarily as the blood lifted from the floor and gyrated into a floating mass. Beans's blood then disappeared into the underpinnings of the hood as though the death-dealer had devoured her life substance. Ham was sure whatever damage Nickl had dealt was now restored.

The death-dealer turned to Nickl and swung its clawed hand two more times. Ham was glad to see each attack miss its target.

Eyeing the candles warily, Ham swallowed hard and stampeded at the death-dealer once more. Three out of four flames hit him this time, bleeding more life from his hit points. He estimated his life to be almost half gone, and he hadn't even damaged the death-dealer. He could not look at his stat sheet. Not yet.

Positioning himself behind the fiend, Ham swung a meaty fist at the back of its head, missing as the death-dealer leaned forward. With a roar, he grabbed the shoulders of the death-dealer and headbutted him in the back of the skull.

The crack was satisfying.

Beans trembled on the opposite side, the deep gash in her cheek dripping blood. "I—I am frozen. He has me stunned from striking me, muley."

"It will go away," Ham assured her. "Just don't go running off!"

The loud crack of an aimed shot echoed in the room, the death-dealer's head snapping back from the impact of the slug. Its hood flew off in the motion, revealing the rotting visage of a hundred-year-old corpse. Brownish decomposing skin slid from muscle, black goop dribbling from the skeleton's mouth and nose. A thick black-and-red striped snake with a triangular head was wrapped around the skull, and the rest of the scaly body disappeared beneath the death-dealer's clothes; it must have wrapped around the body underneath its robes. The snake reared up its head, spinning its attention to Ham.

"*Die... Die...*" the snake hissed through its fangs.

The yellow eyes of the snake were penetrating, hypnotic even, causing Ham to want to turn tail and flee to the far ends of the world. Fear coursed through him, but he stood his ground. The pitter-patter of feet on the opposite side of him told him that Nickl and Beans did not have the same restraint. Upon looking, he noticed they were already out the door of the room and somewhere down the hallway.

Timidly, Ham looked for Kildrak, who returned his gaze with a gapping mouth and wide eyes. He hurried to reload his gun. "I am not going anywhere, Ham. We are going to finish this."

With Nickl gone, it was the death-dealer's turn again. The skeletal creature turned, swiping its clawed hand at Ham. He ducked the attack but didn't see the second one until it had sliced through his belly. Again, time froze as the blood pooled together and levitated in midair until it was eye level with the serpent. Stretching its mouth wide, the snake digested the blood, which seemed to embolden the death-dealer beneath. Gritting his teeth, Ham hurried to swat away the death-dealer's third attack.

The snake suddenly arched and struck, its venomous fangs dripping with anticipation of plunging into Ham's flesh. Quicker than the eye, Ham snapped his head sideways to dodge the attack. He waited for a second attack, but the snake simply coiled back in preparation for its next turn.

"Kill the snake, Ham!" Kildrak shouted.

Unsure how to best the snake, Ham made a tight fist and slammed it downward on top of the snake's head over and over. The first blow clearly dazed the snake; the second one smashed its left eye. Blood trickled from the socket as the snake swayed and hissed.

Kildrak fired his gun again, missing the snake but striking the death-dealer in the back of the shoulder. The bastard lurched forward with a groan.

"Lookin' mighty tangle-footed, *mmhmm.* I think this fight is about over."

In response, the death-dealer weakly swatted at Ham three times, not even coming close to causing any damage. Ham almost laughed at the poor display, when the snake struck again. Its fangs pierced Ham's chest like daggers, venom surging into his muscles. He immediately felt his body weakening, any impact of the blood leaf fleeing from his senses.

He ripped the snake free and roared, stumbling back a step. His sight blurred, but he managed to bring up his stat sheet. He only had twelve hit points left and he was probably poisoned. And he did not remember anyone buying poison antidotes from Mister Sammich.

"Shitfire."

He was going to die.

HAMROGENI "HAM" HERDSTOMPER			LEVEL 4	6700/9000
MEDIUM	MINOTAUR	BARBARIAN	CHAOTIC GOOD	95

POWER	16		HP	12/48
DEXERTITY	14		ARMOR	15
ENDURANCE	14			
INTELLIGENCE	6		SKILLS	SPELLS
AWARENESS	8		INTIMIDATE	IDENTIFY
CHARISMA	4		SURVIVAL	MARKSMAN
LUCK	2		SEAFARING	
			INTERCEPT	
DEFECT	BLOOD LEAF ADDICTION		CHIPS	520

"Ham!"

He barely heard Kildrak's shout before he raged forward and tried to headbutt the snake, or the death-dealer—anything. He nearly fell over in the attempt, striking nothing but air.

Two gunshots exploded from the doorway. "Hang in there, muley!"

Ham tried to see if the bullets killed either the snake or the death-dealer, but he could not make out anything in his foggy state.

"Let's get stabby," he heard Nickl shout as she emerged next to him. Her dark hair was a shadow among the shadows. He heard her blades strike bone again and again.

Another boom sounded as Kildrak fired his gun. A hollow sigh rebounded in Ham's eardrums and then something heavy thudded at Ham's feet. He blinked several times and tried to drown the rushing sound in his ears.

"What is wrong with him?" Nickl asked.

Footsteps approached him on all sides.

"He has been poisoned," Kildrak replied.

"Oh, he will be fine," Beans said. "He took blood leaf, right? It is an antitoxin to snake venom."

"What?" Ham managed to say.

"I took skills in herbalism when I reincarnated last," Beans cooed. "Just give it a minute and you will be fine."

Ham dropped to his knees, surprised when his vision started to clear and the buzzing in his ears dispersed. As Beans suggested, he slowly felt his senses return to normal. Blinking rapidly, he looked up at his friends standing around him and then back to the floor.

The death-dealer lay sprawled out in front of him, and from beneath the robes, he saw the twitching snake. "Oh hell!"

He reached into the mass of cloth and yanked free the

slimy serpent. Warm blood soaked its scales as it wriggled and twisted as though it were making a desperate attempt to slither away.

"It's just the muscles respond—" Nickl tried.

With what strength remained, Ham grabbed the body in either hand and pulled until he ripped the snake in half.

Nickl's hand touched his shoulder. "Ham, I think it was already dead."

"I reckon it's best to be sure, *mmhmm*."

15

The Last Step

The four of them stumbled out of the chamber and into the hallway.

"We need to find a place to rest until dawn and let our wounds heal," Kildrak said. "In the morning, we can travel south again to find Mister Sammich and let him know the deed is done."

Nickl bobbed her head, scanning the corridor ahead. "I agree. Any of these rooms will do just fine."

"If anyone has a liquid blue on 'em..." Ham cleared his throat, feeling the full burden of the wounds on his body, "...I'd welcome a swig or two."

"I got you, muley." Beans's footsteps scraped against the stone behind him. She hurried to find a vial and pushed it into his hand."

"Thank you kindly." Ham gulped down the fluid.

Nickl stopped ahead and pushed open a door to an empty room. Kildrak shoved by her with his gun at the ready; a moment later he shouted an all clear. Ham and Beans reached Nickl's side. Ham peered at the stone floor, almost beckoning him to come lay down and rest.

"Do you think he will return?" Nickl's voice was a squeak at Ham's side.

"The death-dealer?" Ham raised an eyebrow, looking back the way they had come. "I tell you what, if he finds a way to scrape himself off that floor in there, we will knock him back down again, *mmhmm.*"

"You got that right." Beans squeezed by Ham to follow Kildrak into the room.

"H-how is your alignment looking?" Nickl whispered. "If we are going to see Mister Sammich tomorrow, are you going to be al-alright?"

Ham revealed is stat sheet, making it visible to Nickl. His alignment was even higher now than it had been before facing the death-dealer.

Nickl leaped forward and wrapped her arms around his leg with a whelp of delight. "Look at that! You are a good guy, Hamrogeni."

Ham swallowed, staring at his alignment with disbelief. "I reckon so."

She squeezed him again for good measure and walked into the room. Beans and Kildrak had already found a corner to rest. Nickl smiled at them. "Don't worry. I will take first watch."

Ham plopped down against the wall, his stat sheet still hovering in front of him. In the distance, he heard Nickl continuing to talk. Kildrak and Beans added to the conversation.

He could not hear them. He simply sat staring at the numbers until exhaustion finally sent him spiraling into a deep sleep.

It may have been the remnants of the snake's poison or plain exhaustion, but the night hours were a blur.

Ham woke to the sun piercing through the pane glass window of the room in which they had locked themselves. He recalled them each taking a turn to stand lookout—in case anything else untoward remained in the keep—but it was not until the sunbeams hit his pupils that he remembered he was meant to have last watch.

He rubbed the sleep from his eyes and sat up slowly, careful not to make any noise. He hoped to give the impression he had stayed alert while the others slept. He was in the process of straightening his back against the wall when he realized he was alone in the room. The ajar door to his left caused him to gasp.

Nickl, Beans, and Kildrak were no longer with him.

"Oh no..." his voice trailed off.

A moment of panic stung him. He should not have let himself fall asleep in the final hours before daybreak. While his instinct was to rush out the door and down the stairs to find his companions, his body felt frozen against the stone wall. The poison of the snake had fled from his body, yet he felt paralyzed. He fought to find the strength to move, when he realized his friends' bedrolls were missing too. Surely no fiend would kidnap them and take their bedrolls!

He opened his mouth to yell for Nickl when the hum of voices conversing beyond the window touched his ear.

His heart leaped. Half-crawling to the window, he pulled himself up to peek outside. Beyond the wall of Braewood

Keep stood Mister Sammich and, in front of him, Ham saw Nickl, Beans, and Kildrak.

Nickl bounced around in a half-dance, occasionally pumping her fist into the air. Beans grinned from ear to ear, watching Nickl; the blonde-haired gnome pulled out her black-eyed Susans and spun them in a circle before placing them back in their holsters. Kildrak was more stoic, as expected, holding himself up with his pepperbox rifle. He was focused on Mister Sammich, nodding so much his beard was in constant motion against his chest.

Ham could not make out the words.

Relieved that his friends were fine, and the death-dealer had not risen again during the night, Ham sat back on his haunches and smiled. It was time for him to face Mister Sammich too.

He stood up and adjusted his belt before swinging the door open and stepping into the hallway. There, Ham hesitated and turned away from the exit to check on the death-dealer's corpse. He only made it halfway down the corridor before he could see into the room with the pentagram. In the center, the shriveled, bloodied body of the snake lay atop the skeletal remains of the final enemy. Ham nodded with satisfaction. It was really done.

The trek from the tower was swift. Ham took long strides through the narrow passages, leaped several stairs at a time, and dodged the deceased without pause. Soon, he was trotting through the gate of Braewood Keep with the sun—bright as ever—shining on his face. The chatter he heard inside grew louder as he turned the stone corner. In front of him awaited his friends, Mister Sammich, and...Magistrate Charlie in his feathered hat and silken clothes.

"Ham!" Nickl squealed, skipping to his side and hugging his leg. "We did it! The death-dealer is really dead. He didn't come back!"

Ham patted her back with his hand, eyeing the magistrate with caution. He came closer with Nickl still hanging onto his leg. Kildrak nodded to him and Beans waved a hand excitedly in his direction. After offering a respectful nod, Ham focused on the government official. "I reckon you changed your mind and want to arrest us?"

Magistrate Charlie shook his head. "On the contrary, Hamrogeni Herdstomper—"

"You can call me Ham."

"Ham," the magistrate corrected himself. He reached inside of his pocket and pulled up a rolled-up piece of parchment. "I have brought your pardon. You have saved our people from a great horror."

"We are free to go?"

"You can do as you please, Ham. You are a real champion."

A grin split his face. "Darn tootin', I am. But I couldn't have done anything without my friends here, *mmhmm*. They are the ones who delivered the final blows."

Magistrate Charlie dipped his chin in reverence.

Ham drew in a breath, taking in his companions once more. "Well, what now? What do we do?"

Nickl let go of his leg. "That is what we were just discussing, actually, with Mister Sammich."

At mention of his name, the quest-giving shopkeeper stepped forward. "You have reserved the right to become an

NPC. Your alignment and righteous deeds have prepared you to live a good life wherever you please with riches beyond your imagining. On the other hand, you may choose to continue to another adventure either alone or with your friends. You each have your choice to make."

"What have y'all decided then?" Ham asked.

Kildrak shrugged. "Well, I have already chosen to open a small drinking establishment back in Clery and live the NPC life. I am not interested in any more adventuring."

"I would expect nothing less than you running a rum-hole, yammerin' yarns to passersby, dwarf." Ham chuckled as Kildrak's eyes widened. "It will suit you well."

"I need to reach a higher level before I settle down," Beans said, looking into the distance as though she were seeing her future escapades. "You are welcome to go with me, but one way or another, I will be out there shootsing stuff. Be a long while before these guns stop firing."

"I cannot see you doing anything other than raising sand, *mmhmm*," Ham replied before turning to Nickl. "And what about you?"

"I prefer the NPC life, Ham. We have come and gone so many times, working hard to get where we are now. But you know I will go wherever you decide. We are a team, you and me."

He rested his hand on her small shoulder. He looked to the shopkeeper. "What do you reckon I should do? You seem to know everything."

Mister Sammich was stone-faced, speaking almost mechanically as though his script knew no other way to say it. "It is your decision. Do you want to go on another adventure, or are you ready to become a non-player character?"

Hamrogeni Herdstomper
Echoic Mobile Press

Nickl Nackl

Echoic Mobile Press

Kildrak Torunn
Echoic Mobile Press

Beans
Echoic Mobile Press

Death-Dealer

Echoic Mobile Press

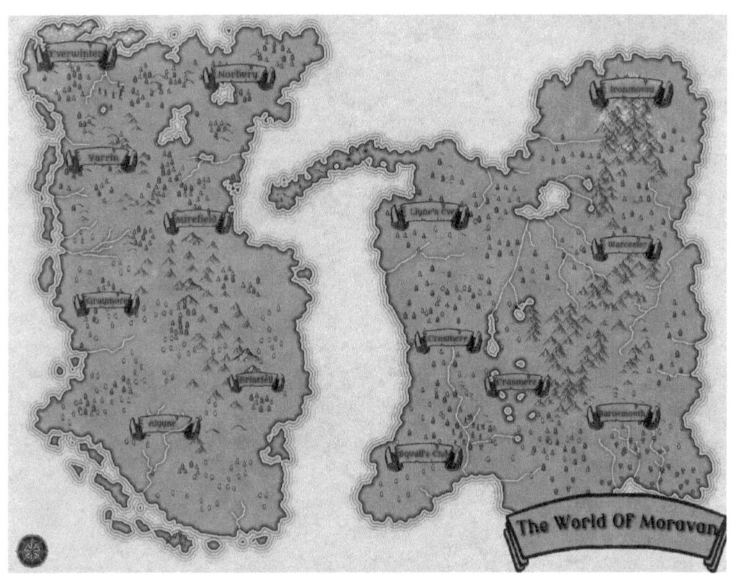

Moravan Map
Echoic Mobile Press